Tom Finder

Martine Leavitt

Red Deer Press

Red Deer Press
813 MacKimmie Library Tower
2500 University Drive N.W.
Calgary Alberta Canada T2N 1N4

Credits
Edited for the Press by Peter Carver
Cover design by Duncan Campbell
Text design by Dennis Johnson
Printed and bound in Canada by Friesens for Red Deer Press

Acknowledgements
Financial support provided by the Canada Council, the Department of
Canadian Heritage, the Alberta Foundation for the Arts, a beneficiary of
the Lottery Fund of the Government of Alberta, and the University of
Calgary.

National Library of Canada Cataloguing in Publication
Leavitt, Martine, 1953–
Tom Finder

ISBN 0-88995-262-0
I. Title. II. Series.
PS8573.E323T65 2003   jC813'.6   C2002-910278-2
PZ7.L3217To 2003

Author's Acknowledgements

My sincere thanks goes to the Canada Council for the Arts and the Alberta Foundation for the Arts, both of which provided financial assistance so I could write this novel. I would also like to thank these people for sharing their wisdom: Ross McInnes and the people at StreetTeams; Mickey at Avenue 15 Shelter for Homeless Youth; Marie and the kids on the Streetlight bus; Colin at Exit Community Outreach; and Jesse at WISH. Thanks also to Kerri Walters, Shawna Cordara, Sarah Bates, Valerie Battrum, and Dr. Keith Spackman for timely help.

A special thank you to Peter Carver, my most excellent editor.

All chapter headings are quoted from *Die Zauberflote (The Magic Flute)*, music by Wolfgang Amadeus Mozart, libretto by Emmanuel Schikaneder, as translated by Susan Webb in *The Metropolitan Opera Book of Mozart Operas*, executive edition (New York: HarperCollins, 1991).

"Words! Theywl move things you know theywl do things. Theywl fetch."

– from *Riddley Walker* by Russell Hoban, Summit Books, New York, 1980

For my Greg

THIS BOOK BELONGS TO TOM FINDER

Chapter 1

Where am I? Is it my imagination that I am still alive?
— Act 1, scene 1

Tom had forgotten who he was.

Something had happened to him, but that was the first thing he forgot. He remembered he had started walking because he couldn't run anymore. His back and rear end hurt all the way through to his stomach.

He forgot if he had a friend as he walked down the steep hill. As the streets became busier he forgot if he'd ever passed Tadpoles, and if he'd ever known what you say to a girl when you like her. By the time the shops began, he forgot what his mark was on his last spelling test, and if he knew what it felt like to get punched in the face, and what his mother looked like. By the time the shops were shadowed by the high downtown towers, he'd forgotten his last name.

No one asked him his name anyway, or looked at him.

He was a little shaky on his feet. Once he bumped into some-one.

"Loser," the person said without looking at him. It was the first thing in the world anyone had ever said to him as far as he knew. He thought it was strange that the person who said it hadn't looked at him.

Tom began to think he was invisible.

He didn't mind. Invisible was good. Maybe if you were invis-ible, gravity had less effect on you. Tom did feel lighter, but that could have been because he hadn't eaten in a while. He'd for-gotten when he'd last eaten, and what it was.

Tom hadn't forgotten his fear of gravity. Or maybe it was new, the newest thing about him since he forgot everything. It was a sensible thing to be afraid of, he thought. Gravity held you down. Sometimes it was so heavy on you that even though you struggled you couldn't get up. He remembered that. He remembered that no matter how hard you try, gravity wins.

He said to himself, *Tom, Tom, Tom* as he walked, so he would-n't forget. He thought that if he forgot that his first name was Tom, he might be invisible even to himself.

Chapter 2

Help! Help! Or else I am lost.
— Act 1, scene 1

The people in the city core thinned out as dusk came on. The streets echoed. They smelled of tar and fries and spilled pop. The smells made his mouth fill up with spit. Tom walked until he came to a paved bike path lined with trees. He had forgotten what day it was—what month it was, for that matter. It was early summer, probably. The leaves on the trees were still a new green. There were people jogging and walking and in-line skating on the path. There were people pushing their babies in strollers. He wondered where they were all going and decided to follow the bike path. He checked his pockets. No money. Probably lost it, like he'd lost his house and his memory.

Loser.

He came to a good place, a river, a mall lit up, a Hard Rock café with people laughing and eating on the balcony. There were geese on the water with their yellow-green babies. He sat on a patch of grass and watched them a long time. He wondered what to do next. There didn't seem to be any next when you didn't have a past. He drew his knees to his chest and rested his elbows on them. He was hungry, and a bit lonely. After a while a woman came out of a nearby condominium with another woman. They glanced at Tom. Only then did Tom realize his patch of grass was a small lawn.

"Why these people gravitate to the best parts of town, I'll never understand," one woman said.

Gravitate.

The massive skyscrapers must have brought him here. He still remembered that the force of gravitational attraction depends on mass: the greater the mass of the two objects, the greater the force pulling them together. Wow. Maybe he was good in science at school.

Tom moved away from the tiny lawn.

He couldn't remember what was in his backpack—maybe a sandwich or a chocolate bar. He looked in. All there was, besides a paperclip and a YOU'RE NICE candy, was a coil notebook.

Tom studied the candy for a long time before he ate it. He hoped it was true, that he was nice, but he couldn't remember.

The notebook could have been a school notebook, but only one page had been written on. The notes were about a guy named Mozart. He didn't remember making the notes.

Johannes Chrystostomus Wolfgangus Theophilus Mozart
– Wolfgang Amadeus for short
– genius musishan, cumposer
– played for the Emperor at age 5, Emperor called him "little magishan"

Tom studied the notes as if they were a map back to somewhere. Strange that in the forgetting he'd remembered how to spell. M–A–G–I–C–I–A–N.

He closed the book and looked in the pack again.

No pen. He thought he'd like to write his name—Tom, Tom, Tom—just in case. It might be good to write things down about himself in case he started forgetting again, but no pen. He must have been one of those disorganized students.

"Tom, why aren't you working on your assignment?"

"I don't have a pen, sir."

Yeah. Maybe he'd write that down, too, when he had a pen. Maybe that was a memory.

He crossed the bridge, away from the mall and the condominiums. Across the bridge was a park. He made it to a bench by the river before his knees gave up. He supposed he should go to the police, tell them he had amnesia or whatever it was, but he felt safe as long as he was invisible. Going to the police would definitely make him visible. Maybe he'd go tomorrow.

He watched the river running. He lay down and positioned his backpack under his head. He thought he would close his eyes for a minute. He didn't mean to sleep.

Tom woke from the cold in the night, but he didn't move or open his eyes. He lay still and listened to the river. As long as he could feel the notebook under his head, he felt safe. It was a clue to remembering who he was. He went back to sleep.

The next time he woke up, it was light out and he could hear moaning. The moaning stopped, but Tom's blood was electric. He lay still. When the moaning started again, he sat up. The bench and the river and the park were inside a cloud of fog.

More moaning.

Tom stood. He took a few steps, following the sound until he saw someone standing on the bank by the river. He went closer. It was a big man with black and silver braids and a big, brown, pitted face. He wore a fringed leather jacket with beads on the fringes which clicked as he rocked from side to side. Now the moaning sounded like it might be a plea for help.

"Hey. Are you okay?" Tom called from where he was. His legs were so shaky that he wasn't sure he could run fast enough if the man chased him.

The man slowly looked around.

He fixed his eyes on Tom. He could see him. The man looked up at the sky, then back to Tom. "This is my answer?" he said aloud. "A pretty white boy?"

"Do you need any help?" Tom asked. He hoped the man would say, no, get out of here kid, and then Tom would go and see if anyone was looking for him. He hoped his parents were rich. He'd ask them to take him to Mickey D's on the way home. The man looked at Tom like the very sight of him was disappointing. He said nothing and seemed to look at something behind Tom. Tom needed to find a toilet. He turned away to see that there were people standing around him. Boys, some as young as him, each wearing a leather jacket. One turned around as if on lookout. On the back of his jacket was a red dragon.

"Hi," Tom said, because of what the candy had said.

One of them took a step toward Tom and smiled as if he only wanted to show his teeth. Tom couldn't run. "You got toys in that pack?" he asked Tom.

The silver-braided man emerged from the fog like a ghost. "Leave him," he said. His beads clicked in a breeze Tom could not feel.

They ignored the older man. One, and then another, took his hands out of his pockets.

"All I've got is a notebook," Tom said.

It wasn't their fists he was afraid of, it was their eyes. They could see him. He wondered if in his forgotten life he could fight.

"Leave him alone," the man said again, though no more loudly.

This time they looked at the older man. One of them ran his thumb along the sharp edge of his front teeth, then pointed his thumb at Tom, smiled, and walked away. The others followed. Tom's knees unlocked, and he sat heavily on the bench. The older man sat beside him.

"Thanks," Tom said to the man after a minute.

The man nodded slowly. "You can repay me. I prayed for a Finder, and you found me."

Nothing the man said made any sense to Tom. He hoped he wasn't forgetting English. The man held out his huge hand.

"Samuel Wolflegs. I am looking for my son, Daniel. Do you know him? Have you seen him?" His voice was deep and trembly, as if his lungs were shaking at their roots.

"No," Tom said.

The man took a picture out of his pocket, a small school photograph. "This boy. This is the one I'm looking for. Daniel Wolflegs."

Tom shook his head, but the man held out the photograph as if he expected Tom to take it. Finally, Tom put the photograph in the pocket of his hood.

"What's your name, white boy?" the man asked.

Tom pulled his hood over his head. "Tom," he said.

"Tom what?"

Tom shrugged. "Tom nothing. Tom."

"What are you doing here?" the man asked. "School get out early for you? Most kids have a few days left."

Tom thought about that a moment. He hoped he wasn't skipping school. He was pretty sure he wasn't that kind of kid.

"You are lost. Strange, for a Finder to be lost. Do you know where you are?"

Tom looked around and shook his head.

"Prince's Island," the man said. "The river gave you to me, for an answer to my praying."

Tom thought probably he should run away, but his feet had already died of starvation. If he was going to die, he was glad it would be from the feet up and not from the head down. His brain must have already lost weight, though, because he thought he could feel it slosh around in his skull.

"Look, I'm just a kid, okay? Just a loser kid . . ." He stood up. His stomach was so empty and light that it was defying gravity.

"Not a loser. A Finder," Wolflegs said.

Tom began to stump away on dead feet.

"What's that blood on your jeans?" Wolflegs asked. "On the back of your jeans?"

Tom stopped. He craned his neck around to see. "I . . . I forget," he said.

"Let me take you to a doctor," Samuel Wolflegs said.

Tom shook his head once. The world vibrated. He couldn't explain how he needed to be invisible right now.

Wolflegs had the still look of a hunter after wary prey.

"If you walk around like that, someone is going to notice. Why don't you go for a swim in the river? If the blood washes off and there's no more fresh blood, then okay."

Tom thought about it for a minute, then stripped off his hoodie and walked into the river. The water was cold, but he got used to it quickly. He relieved himself in it. He swam in it, hidden by the white fog, invisible, buoyed up against gravity.

When he came out of the water, Wolflegs was sitting with his arms folded over his chest, scanning the river up and down as if he were on the lookout. The fog was white in the morning light; the geese were honking. Tom shivered, but the day was going to be warm.

"Good swimmer," Wolflegs said.

Tom wondered if he had always been a good swimmer. His parents must have put him in swimming lessons as a kid.

"Well, see ya," Tom said. He felt better, enough to walk again.

"You will look for my son, Daniel," Samuel called, commanding Tom from the roots of his lungs. There was a deep sadness in his voice that kept Tom from running away.

Tom turned to him and said, "Look, I'm not a Finder, whatever that is—"

"You are. I say you have the power. I see it in you."

"I don't believe in that stuff." He couldn't remember if he didn't believe in that stuff.

"That's what Daniel said." Wolflegs said. He began to weep silently. The tears pooled in the acne scars on his face. "He came to the streets because we fought. He wouldn't respect the old ways. I called him a McIntosh, an apple, red on the outside, white on the inside. I threw him out. I locked the door. He came here, found people who took him into the cult of the street. When I walk the streets looking for him, they hide him from me. They say they don't know where he is, they haven't seen him. Tell him I am here, I say, where the bridge crosses the river. Tell him

I am sorry for the things I said. Tell him all is forgotten." He was silent for a moment. "But I have been here a long time, and Daniel does not come." The man turned away from Tom and gazed at the river. "If he came back to me, I would give him the river. With the river everything can be new again."

"Go to the police," Tom said.

"I have. I have gone so many times that they threaten to detain me if I come again. Public nuisance, they say. They imitate my talk. We don't look for runaways, they say. He's a big boy, they say."

"I will stay by the river, praying, until you find him."

He started praying again, a sound somewhere between singing and moaning. His eyes closed. *Weird*, Tom thought as he began walking away. *How can you give someone a river?*

"Sleep here and you will be safe," the man called. Before Tom was out of earshot, Wolflegs called to him again: "Don't follow the streets. They never take you where you want to go. Especially at night. They keep you. Get up with the sun, Tom Finder . . ."

Tom started out by looking for a police officer. He hit the jackpot and found city police headquarters. He walked toward the stone stairs that led to the entranceway, and then walked by. His mind must have been elsewhere, he thought, and he turned and walked back. Again he marched right on by. Tom looked down at his feet as if they'd grown a mind of their own. He shook his head, walked toward the stairs, and walked by again.

This was ridiculous. Perhaps whatever had made him lose his memory had caused some sort of brain damage as well. This time he forced his feet to stop at the stone stairs. He felt it. Gravity was pushing him away. Not just any old gravity, but high-density, collapsed-star-type gravity, the kind that squeezed all the food out of your stomach if there was any in it. He quickly walked away. He'd come back later.

Tom got on an LRT train. He rode for a long time. He got off where he had started, in the downtown core. He rode another route for a couple of hours. He looked out the window at the houses, wondering who lived there, how they had picked that house in that spot. Each one was a hiding place, a place to be invisible, to do all your private acts. He rode standing up. He stared at the houses. Sometimes, if the curtains were open, he could see in, see children watching TV or people sitting at the table. They were just glimpses, like postcards.

He felt a huge sadness inside, this big, empty, locked-out feeling, like everything good had to happen in a house, like all of life happened in houses and no one would let him in and he didn't even know how to ask. He liked the little houses as well as the big ones. He would have been happy to call any one of them home, but none looked familiar.

Just as the train headed into the core, a uniformed man approached Tom. Just feeling his eyes on him made Tom have to struggle for air.

A black kid in the seat across the aisle said, "Uh-oh. Here come the Tallyman."

Tom looked blankly at the boy.

"TC. Train cop," the black kid said in a loud whisper without looking at him.

TC was barrel-chested and big-bellied. He had a huge head and thick arms, but his legs were long and skinny. He looked like he should topple over, top-heavy. He stopped in front of Tom.

"Ticket?"

Tom had forgotten about tickets.

He held out his hands and shrugged. The black kid sighed across the aisle as the train cop took a pen and book out of the inside pocket of his jacket.

"Name?"

"Tom."

"Tom what?"

Tom shrugged.

"Tom Shrug?" The man laughed at his own joke and looked around good-naturedly at the other passengers. "How old are you, Tom Shrug?"

Tom shrugged again. TC stared. He glanced again at the other passengers and bit his pen with big yellow teeth.

"You look about fourteen, fifteen? What's your address?" He settled his face into a frown.

Tom didn't answer. Everyone on the train was looking at him. Being seen was making him nauseous. He was glad there was nothing inside his stomach.

"Look kid, you cooperate, all you get is a fine. Give me trouble, and I can have you arrested. Now, where do you live?"

"I forget," Tom said. The black kid snickered.

The train cop put his pen in its clip. "Forget to buy a ticket, too?"

Tom nodded, relieved that the man understood.

The train cop grabbed Tom's collar and jerked him from his seat. "Come on, you little snot—"

The black kid said, "Hey, Mr. Tallyman. Be cool." He was smiling; his voice was cajoling.

"Just let me do my job," Train Cop said.

"Look. Here, I pay the ticket," the kid said.

"Too late," TC said. He pulled Tom by his shirt down the aisle. "At this point you'd have to pay his fine."

The black kid stood up. "Okay, Mr. Tallyman. Jus' be easy on the cloth." Standing, he came up to TC's shoulder. TC ignored him and began dragging Tom off the train. Tom felt his shirt tear. TC seemed to defy gravity. His huge torso shouldn't be able to balance on those long, wobbly legs, let alone pull Tom around like he weighed nothing.

The black kid grabbed TC's arm. "Man, what your badge number?"

TC's grip eased on Tom just for a moment, just long enough to push the kid, long enough for Tom to get away.

He ran.

He didn't run—he raced!

He must have been a track star in school—fast, fast, fast. Train Cop couldn't catch him. What's-your-name couldn't catch him. How-old-are-you-where-do-you-live couldn't catch him . . . maybe not even gravity itself . . .

The black kid was running beside him, laughing and flapping his arms. Tom sped up and lost him. Lost him, and then Tom himself was safely lost and invisible again.

Tom ran until his legs remembered they had died of malnutrition, and then he walked.

He walked a long time among the downtown workers, his head just beneath the level of their gaze. Tom observed the way the downtown workers walked, straight-backed and purposeful. Most wore black and carried briefcases, both the men and the women. He liked to look at them. They looked fresh, as if they'd been wrapped in plastic wrap all night as they slept. He wondered what was in their briefcases. Maybe a ham sandwich or a chocolate bar. Most likely just papers, like in his backpack.

Only one person looked at him. A girl, pale and rumpled and overweight, was standing near the Jigglety Bumps Daycare. From a distance she watched the mothers bringing their children to the daycare. She stared at each baby. Her face was intent, her eyes as hungry as his stomach. Then she turned her gaze to Tom. She saw him. Tom quickly walked away.

If he were a Finder, like Samuel Wolflegs said, if there were any such thing, he would find himself food.

And maybe a pen.

Yeah. A pen. So he could write down his name, which was Tom, and that he was nice. Probably nice.

Tom looked for a pen. What could it hurt? He was walking anyway. He looked in the cracks of the sidewalk and in the street gutter. He looked under the benches and around the bus shelters. He looked in the token flower beds and on the window ledges of the tall buildings. He looked under statues and peeked into garbage cans. There was no pen.

That's because it was in his hoodie pocket.

He rubbed his stomach where it felt empty and sore, and he felt it in there.

Weird.

Tom took it out of his pocket and looked at it. It said, CALGARY OPERA. MOZART'S *THE MAGIC FLUTE.*

Weird.

Tom sat on a bench and pulled out the notebook and read again the notes on Mozart.

Someone had scribbled in the margin—probably him—as if he were writing to another student: **Eye balls are freeky,** and **Louise sizles, ouch, ouch, ouch,** and **This Mozart guy was real. Gonna see one of his opras.** *Opera,* Tom thought. O–P–E–R–A.

Tom thought for a moment about throwing the notes away, then changed his mind. Somehow they were important; somehow they connected him with his life before the Forgetting. Instead, on a fresh page, he wrote his name: **Tom.**

He looked at it for a little while. He realized he could make up a last name if he wanted. He could write anything he wanted in that notebook. He could write **2 + 2 = 5** if he wanted. He could write a story about himself being a fine swimmer and a fast runner and a Finder. He could write a story about a prince, Prince Tom, who rescues a fair maiden . . .

Tom wrote: **Something happened to Tom, but that was the first thing he forgot. Too bad, because Tom, he was a nice guy.**

A dog sniffed at Tom's shoes. He patted the dog's head. He must be visible to animals. The dog must have been able to tell that Tom hadn't been near food for a long time because he moped away. Tom thought of following him, of sharing whatever the dog could sniff out, then went back to looking at what he had just written in his notebook. His pen-lines were wobbly. His fingers were starting to die of starvation.

He was about to write something else when he heard a screech of brakes in front of him, and a *thud.*

A car had hit the dog. A man emerged halfway from his car, looked, and drove away.

Tom shoved the notebook into his backpack and ran to kneel by the dog. He thought it might still be breathing.

"It's okay, dog," he said, gently patting its side. He looked around and saw a pay phone. He didn't have money, but he thought maybe 911 was free. He ran and dialed. He remembered 911; he just couldn't remember exactly what it was for.

"911."

"I'm not sure this is the number I should be calling, but there's a dog run over, corner of . . . um . . . MacLeod and Seventh."

"The number you are calling from, sir?"

"I don't know. It's a pay phone."

"We'll contact the SPCA for you, sir. They'll want to know what kind of dog it is."

"I don't know." He'd forgotten his dog species.

"The SPCA will want to know what kind of dog it is, sir."

"I don't know. Flat. A flat dog. It might still be alive." Tom dropped the phone. He ran back to the dog. It was panting rapidly. Its back legs were lying at a wrong angle to the rest of its body. Its eyes were open, afraid.

"Hey, boy. Someone's coming," Tom said gently. He thought he remembered how it felt to be run over by gravity, pressed flat and twitching. He thought he could remember that.

In a little while a small crowd gathered, and soon after that a policeman tapped him on the shoulder.

"You the one who made the crank call to 911?"

"He's still alive," Tom said. He placed his hand on the dog's head.

"That's what happens when you tackle the pavement," the officer said. "Pavement always wins. Come with me, boy. The SPCA is coming, but we're going to have to pay your parents a visit and get them to teach you the appropriate use of 911."

The dog raised its head, and Tom stood up.

"Just leave the nice kid alone," someone in the crowd said to the officer.

Tom looked around. They were all looking at him. Seeing him. Suddenly, nausea hit his stomach like a fist. He swayed on his feet. No. Not nausea—hunger. He felt hungry with their eyes on him, and he was suddenly aware that his hair hadn't been combed and his teeth were scummy.

"Come on, kid. I'll give you a ride home," the officer said.

"That's okay," Tom said, swallowing.

"I insist."

"I don't know where home is," Tom said.

The officer's face closed over that. "Well, then, we'll just have to go down to the station and see if we can't help you remember." Somehow it didn't seem like a friendly offer.

They were all looking at him, around him, and he was visible. He felt the skin on his scalp clench up.

Tom ran. His feet and knees were dead of starvation, but his thighs worked, and he ran. He ran until his thighs died and the only thing left alive in him was his stomach, and it was crying.

He leaned against a wall. It was him crying. He told himself it was for the dog, and he stopped as soon as he could.

For one scary moment he thought he was forgetting his first name, too. He tore the notebook out of his backpack and opened it up. **Tom. Nice guy.** He stared at it until his breathing returned to normal. He pulled the pen out of his pocket. He looked closely at it. Besides the printing, the pen had a dragon on it, and a birdlike creature. He wanted to write something. He had to write something. He could write anything he wanted. But what? What?

Tom wrote, **Tom found food.** He read it over several times, then put the pen and notebook in his backpack.

He would have tried panhandling if he hadn't needed to be invisible. He walked until the skyscrapers ended and the shops began: art stores, bookstores, banks, insurance brokers, real estate offices, law offices, boutiques, coffee shops. Tom stopped outside a fast-food chicken place. The smell almost pushed him over, but he knew people would look at him if he fell. He wondered whether it was considered robbery if you used a pen in your pocket to hold up a store. Tom thought for a while, then walked around the block and checked out the dumpster behind the store. A batch of burnt chicken lay among the other garbage. He glanced around. It was quiet there in between the dumpster and the wire fence. No one would see. He reached in.

He had never tasted anything so delicious in his whole life. At least, not that he could remember.

He'd found food.

"Tom Finder," he said aloud to himself between mouthfuls. Weird.

Tom put down the chicken long enough to write **Tom was a Finder** in his notebook. He put the book away, along with three wings which he was going to save for later.

He walked again. People looked at him if he stopped in one place very long. His stomach couldn't tolerate that. He needed water. He walked until the shops turned into tiny dirty houses, and the small landscaped spaces between buildings became yards full of weeds and junked cars. Some of the houses had plastic sheeting instead of glass in the windows, and others had blankets for curtains. The roofs sagged like they were going to fall in. It seemed strange to Tom that the skyscrapers, which should be too heavy for the earth to hold up, rose up as light as foil and bubble, defying gravity, while these little houses sagged under the weight of the air.

A man stumbled out the front door of his house and puked beside the porch. Tom stopped. Should he ask if he was okay? The man straightened and looked at him.

"Get off my property!" he bellowed, staggering toward him.

Tom ran. The guy could see him! It made Tom's belly hurt to see the guy coming at him. He ran, back to the Core, back to the skyscrapers and the people dressed in black, whose faces and clothes weren't crushed by the air, whose gaze was above his head. Tom ran until he was safe and invisible.

By the time the sun went behind the skyscrapers, Tom had five blisters on his feet. The backs of his knees felt bruised, and he clumped along as if he had sticks for legs. Everyone was going home, or leaving the Core at least—the beautiful downtown workers who looked as if they belonged in aquariums with special lighting. They hadn't seen him all day, and no wonder. Maybe it wasn't that he was invisible. Maybe they were too busy feasting their eyes on their beautiful each others.

Tom didn't want to go back to the river. Samuel Wolflegs, medicine man, might be there. At dusk he found a bridge to hide under. Like a bug under a rock, he thought. He was so cold that he didn't think he could sleep, but he was dozing when someone woke him up shouting.

"Ghosts! Ghosts!" The voice echoed under the bridge. In the dim light Tom could see an old man.

Someone yelled, "Shut up!" and Tom heard a bottle smash.

"Can't you see them?" the old man wailed. "Ghosts everywhere."

Someone chucked another bottle at the old guy, and his voice dropped to a whimper.

"Leave him alone," Tom, nice guy, called out.

Another bottle landed, this one so close to the old guy that glass sprayed over him. Tom leaped up and went to stand beside him. He looked around at the people littering the underbelly of the bridge. He heard low laughter. "Lucky I'm outta bottles," someone called, "but I'm working on another here."

"C'mon," Tom said to the old man. He grabbed the old guy's elbow and led him out from under the bridge until they stood directly under a streetlight.

"Are you a ghost?" the old man asked Tom.

"No," Tom said. At least he didn't think so. Ghosts didn't feel this thirsty. "Do you have somewhere else you can go?"

"Nowhere to go, just like them," the old man said. He had a small head, shrunken, as if it had been left out to dry too long. He wore a red cap that said, IF YOU THINK I'M CUTE YOU SHOULD SEE MY MOMMY. He looked around a lot, as if he felt himself being touched.

"I'll take you home," Tom said.

The man looked at him in terror. "You are a ghost. You've come for me, to take me. But not yet, not yet . . ."

The man scurried away, looking back twice to see if Tom was chasing him. The streets echoed. Tom was alone, but he didn't feel alone anymore. He could feel his body hair itching his legs and arms and neck.

He went back to the bridge, but a bottle smashed at his feet. Tom turned around and clumped back to the river.

He wondered if Samuel Wolflegs would still be there. The guy creeped him out, but at least he could sleep safely there.

Wolflegs had been right about one thing: the streets hadn't taken him anywhere he wanted to go. But that was today. Tomorrow . . . *Clump, clump.* His feet burned. Strange that all these flat streets and level roads could bend to a round earth. There had to be places where it ended, where a road traveler had to fall off the edge, then begin again until the curve became too much.

At the bridge he stopped and looked down at the river for a long time. Wolflegs had said he wanted to give his son Daniel the river. You couldn't own a river even if you were rich, but at that moment Tom wished he could. Just looking at the river made him feel better, made his thirst less angry, and his blisters less sting-y. He hadn't noticed that about rivers before, how they flowed through you and washed your heart and head from the inside. It was like giving his brain a drink. Or maybe he had noticed before, and he'd just forgotten.

Tom walked over the bridge without seeing Wolflegs. He walked to the far side of the park, out of the carefully landscaped grounds into the brush. He'd come to another branch of the river. He was on an island, created by two arms of the river. Tom explored his island. He didn't know what he was looking for, but he was earnestly seeking it.

He found a blanket hanging in a tree.

He went closer. There were spiderwebs attaching it to the branch it hung on. It must have been there for a while. He took it down. It was thick and soft, and not so used. Tom shook it out and lay it in the underbrush by the river. He took out his note-book and pen and wrote, **Tom lives on Prince's Island.** Just in case he forgot. He could write a story if he wanted, about how he was a prince, about how he would find a fair maid to rescue. Tom wrote it down.

Weird.

He was starting to creep himself out now.

"Loser," he said to himself.

The sound of it frightened him. There was so little of him to know that that one word took up a lot of room in himself. He took out his notebook and read his previous entry: **Finder.** Not a loser. A Finder. Wolflegs had said.

He wrapped himself in his blanket and tried to sleep.

Chapter 3

If he isn't going to be afraid of me soon, I will run away.
— Act 1, scene 2

What? Am I to feed on stones?
— Act 1, scene 3

"Hey, Tom Finder. Sleeping rough again, eh?"

Samuel Wolflegs was sitting beside him. He was the first thing Tom saw when he opened his eyes. "Did you find my boy, Daniel?"

"No," Tom said. He clutched the blanket around himself, rolled over, and closed his eyes.

"Don't feel bad. He is a wolf, wild on the streets, lone, a little dangerous. You found a blanket, though. Good."

Tom had had enough sleep to see how finding the blanket could have been a coincidence. He kept his eyes closed. As for the pen, technically he hadn't found it, since he'd had it all along.

"Up with the sun, boy. Don't lose the rhythms of the earth. That's the first step to letting the street have you. You don't want her to have you. She's a bad mother, or worse."

"I'm tired. Go away."

"Bet you're hungry."

Tom rolled back and looked at Wolflegs.

"Got an egg salad sandwich here if you're awake."

Tom sat up. "Okay, I'm awake."

Wolflegs held out the wrapped sandwich. Tom's hands shook as he unwrapped it. He was so thirsty that he didn't think there was any spit left in him, but some came. He ate the whole thing in six bites.

"You're here early," Tom said with his mouth full. "Don't you go home at night?"

"My son did not sleep in a bed last night, so I do not," Wolflegs said.

Tom's throat was so dry that he swallowed with difficulty. "I'm gonna drink that river now," he said.

Wolflegs shook his head. "That's white man's water. You haven't had anything to drink?"

"There's no fountains anywhere."

"Some of the buildings have washrooms open to the public. They have fountains for the tourists."

"Where do the tourists go?"

"Come. I'll show you."

Tom folded his blanket over a branch. He was afraid to walk in the Core with someone as tall as Samuel Wolflegs, with someone who had long black and silver braids, with someone who for sure would be seen. But his thirst was greater than his fear.

He needn't have feared.

"They don't see you either," Tom said as they walked.

"They don't want to," Wolflegs said. "Chicken skins, all of them."

"I think they are pretty. They look good—I mean, they look like they would be good."

Wolflegs grunted. "Money can make you look moral."

Tom wondered what he meant. "How long have you been looking for Daniel?" He needed to talk to take his mind off his thirst, though his speech sounded sticky.

"Since last winter," Wolflegs said. "He's left before, when we fought. But this time demons got him."

"Demons?"

"Bad medicine. Demons. They say drugs made him crazy, but it was his demons made him take the drugs. It was demons made him take more and more. Some say he's dead. He's not dead. If he was dead, I would have seen his ghost."

"There's no such thing as demons."

Wolflegs looked at him. "That's what Daniel said. He didn't know about demons, about bad magic, and so he wouldn't use the good magic I had to give him."

"Good magic, eh?" Tom said. He tried to smile, but his cheeks didn't work. He tried again. Nothing. He guessed he'd forgotten how to smile, too. "You mean magic like the power I have to be a Finder?" He would have laughed if his cheeks had worked and his throat wasn't as dry as the sidewalk.

"Yes, like that," Samuel said.

Tom said nothing. His legs were stiff and his tongue coated, and he was walking beside a medicine man who believed in magic, and if gravity had a thumb he was sure it was pressing down on him right now.

"You should find your way home," Wolflegs said almost gently. "I am wrong to keep you here, looking for Daniel."

Tom almost said, "Don't worry, I'm not looking for Daniel," but something stopped him. He didn't know many things about himself, but he knew he was "nice." The candy had said so, and now it was written down in his notebook. Nice was pretty vague. How good did you have to be to be nice? Did you just have to not say mean things? Or did you have to find people's kids for them?

"Where is home for you, Tom?" Samuel asked.

"I don't know," Tom said. "But when I see it, I guess I'll know."

Wolflegs looked at him. For a while he didn't say anything. Then, "You forget everything?"

Tom nodded.

"You forgot on purpose."

Tom shook his head once.

"How'd you forget?"

"I forget." He might have smiled, but the corner of his lips could hardly defy this kind of gravity.

Wolflegs turned Tom to the right and pointed. "The Calgary Tower. There are fountains in here for the tourists. And I've got money to take you to the top. Come on."

At the fountain Tom slurped and guzzled until his stomach rounded out, then he drank a little more.

Wolflegs led Tom into the elevator. "My son grew up in a box, in a square house with square rooms, and in the day he went to a square box school. No wonder he came here, to this place, where everything is boxes, only big. The god of boxed things lives here." He grunted. "Boxes are good for coffins."

On their way up in the elevator, Wolflegs droned on, and Tom only half-listened to him talking about stars and what they looked like when he was a child, so many stars that there was no space between them. Tom was sure he could feel the lower gravity as they went higher and higher. It felt good.

"Worst part of being on the streets is boredom," Wolflegs said. "No school, no chores, no job. Feels good at first, then it gets boring. Drugs fill in the boredom, but they make you more bored, and soon you're so bored that you want to die and so boring that nobody cares if you do. Stay close to the earth, Tom Finder. Sleep near the river; learn from it. Sit near trees, on green grass. Be like a weed that pushes up through the pavement and cracks the sidewalk."

Tom's stomach sloshed and gurgled as the elevator came to a stop. The elevator doors opened.

Wolflegs kept talking, but Tom didn't hear him at all anymore. The whole city lay like a map below him. It was still, as if no people lived in it. If you looked closely you could see cars moving, but they moved slowly and silently.

Tom walked from window to window, pressing his face against them, examining the neighborhoods and landmarks to see if he remembered anything. Nothing was familiar. It was when Tom looked almost straight down that he saw something he was looking for.

It was a billboard. On it was a strange birdlike creature, and the words, THE MAGIC FLUTE, SEPTEMBER 12–15. It made him feel a little sick to his stomach to look at it, or maybe he was afraid of heights since the Forgetting. Maybe before, too. There was no way to know. That opera, though, had something to do with home, with who he was. Maybe his mom worked there in ticket sales or something. His parents probably weren't rich. They probably lived in an ordinary house and had two ordinary cars and worked at ordinary jobs. Maybe his dad was a welder, or a science teacher. His mom probably coached swimming in her spare time. She must have been the one who taught him to swim. They probably missed him like Samuel missed his son, Daniel.

Maybe he'd rent a billboard like that to let his parents know where he was.

"I might have found a way to find my parents," Tom said. He noticed an electronic sign across the street that said JUNE 27.

Wolflegs didn't answer. He was looking too, trying to see the almost invisible people below. "Your power is given to help others. You will only be a Finder if you look for my Daniel." His fingertips and nose were touching the viewing glass. There was a wolf in his eye.

"Do you see him?"

"No," Wolflegs said. He stepped back from the glass, and his eyes lost their animal gleam.

They waited for the elevator in silence. On the way down Wolflegs didn't look at him. The tears were streaming down his face again. They filled the acne scars on his stony face and streamed onto his black and gray braids. Tom wished he could remember who would be looking for him, maybe crying for him like this. Finding Daniel would be a fair trade for finding home.

"I'll find Daniel," Tom said.

Wolflegs looked at Tom with his lone-wolf eyes, yellow, searching, wolfy eyes. "I gave you the gift. I named it in you. You must use it to find Daniel first. You won't find home until you find Daniel."

The elevator stopped and they got out. Tom had another long drink at the fountain.

"I'll be at the river," Wolflegs said before he strode away.

Tom looked for money for the pay phone. He found a quarter, a dime, a nickel, and four pennies under bus benches. He called Bill's Billboards. He found out that to rent a billboard for four weeks cost $2,700. It also cost $4 per square foot for producing a design. That made a total of $5,388. Tom put the nickel and four pennies in his pocket. Now he only needed $5,387.91.

The next day Tom found food in a dumpster behind a bakery: day-old rye bread and a squashed cream puff. Later that morning he found an unlocked washroom at a Fas Gas where he washed himself, and still later he found a Sally Ann drop-off, where he found a clean pair of socks. For lunch he found a box of brown, bruised bananas behind a Safeway. He ate three and saved a few for later.

Wherever he went he looked for Daniel Wolflegs. He saw no wolves, no warriors.

He didn't mind looking. When his parents found him, they'd take him out of the Core's orbit. Looking for Daniel meant he was on his way home, headed that way, only on foot: slower than a car, but faster than a house. One day he'd get to where the sky-scrapers ended, and then a little farther, and then he'd know who he was.

He rode the trains and buses, looking for Daniel. He was not invisible to Train Cop. As soon as he saw him, Tom got off and ran. Sometimes he just sat in the stations. They were one of the best places to find stuff.

Tom wondered at times if the things he found were some sort of communication between him and the skyscraping workers, the beautiful mannequins come alive. It was as if they were say-ing to him, "Here, boy, have some gum. Here, boy, have a toonie and a pair of sunglasses. Here, boy, noticed your hair's messy; have a comb. No teeth missing, just a few bent ones. Here, boy, have a packet of licorice, a *People* magazine, a bologna sandwich, a broken skateboard, a can of pop with only a few sips gone."

Tom used the first toonie he found to buy a toothbrush. After that he made a deal with a guy named Tuba at the Greyhound bus station. Tom got the slightly bent locker in exchange for cleaning out the lockers once a week. He was proud of himself for striking the deal and figured maybe his dad was a businessman and he took after him. He didn't like carrying everything he found. It increased his mass, made it easier for gravity to find him. Besides, he'd discovered that the richer you were, the less you carried. The poor had shopping carts, and the rich had thin briefcases, the thinner the richer.

Tom discovered a place that would pay him for discarded pop bottles and cans. He saved all his money in his locker. He only needed $5,364 more. He tried never to spend money on food.

One morning, as he was going through the bakery garbage, he noticed someone looking at him. When you were invisible, you could feel eyes on you.

A man wearing white pants and a dirty apron was standing at the back door. "Get out of my garbage," he said.

"Why?" Tom asked.

"Because I'll call the cops if you don't."

"Have you got plans for this garbage?"

The man turned around to go back into the store. Tom grabbed two handfuls of muffins and ran.

After that the baker mashed everything together before he threw it out. Tom learned to like the taste of pumpkin pie on his sausage roll, and not to mind his bread smeared with lemon tart like it was jam.

One day he went into Future Shop, to see if they had bottles and cans, and also to see what they sold there. As soon as he walked in, he knew that something from home was here, something that was true about him. Then he knew it was television. There were dozens of them, maybe hundreds, all tuned to the same channel. He counted them. One hundred and thirty-eight.

He remembered the closing credits of this show. The closing

credits of "McCullough Avenue." He had them memorized. He remembered the characters in it—the names of each family member. There was Judith and Raymond McCullough and their three children. He knew the show's song off by heart. He remembered that Raymond, the father, was funny. You could never be too sad or mad with a dad like that. You'd spend your whole life just cracking up. He loved Judith the mom. He wanted to kiss the screen just looking at her. She was an advertising executive, but she never seemed to go to work. She took her kids to swimming lessons and sat with them while they practiced piano and had long talks with them over homemade cookies. The oldest McCullough kid, Trevor, was funny like his dad. He made his kid sister feel smart, and he was a good friend to Beaner next door. Trevor McCullough was nice.

News.

Tom watched, hoping someone had reported a lost boy.

There was no lost boy reported, but he came again the next day. He came every day to watch the news and hoped that "McCullough Avenue" would be on.

Sometimes he listened to music while he was there.

"Got any Mozart?" Tom asked the clerk one day after he'd spent time staring at the notes in his notebook.

"Sorry. All out," the clerk said, focusing his eyes on a grease stain on Tom's shirt.

A few days later, after he had found a clean shirt at the Sally Ann drop-off bin, Tom asked again. "Got any Mozart?"

This time the clerk looked in his eyes. Tom's throat closed. "You're hanging around here too much," the clerk said.

Tom stayed away from the Future Shop for a while, until one day he woke up and knew he couldn't stay away any longer. He was sure that if he listened to Mozart, he'd remember something that would remind him of home.

On the way he stopped before the MAGIC FLUTE billboard. Someone had pinned a handwritten sign to it: **Find God.** Tom wondered if he had believed in God before the Forgetting. He wondered if God were playing some sort of cosmic hide-and-seek, which didn't seem fair since God could make Himself invisible if He wanted. If a guy was a Finder, though, that would make the game easier. If he were an invisible Finder, that would definitely even up the game a little. Samuel was so sure he was a Finder that sometimes Tom believed him. After a long day of searching and not finding Daniel or home, he knew it couldn't be true. Still, there was the pen, and the blanket, and the food.

The Future Shop was closed, and while he was waiting for the store to open Tom noticed the church next door had its door propped.

He figured that was likely a good place to look for God.

Tom peeked in. Before his eyes could adjust to the dark, he heard a man say, "Come in."

Tom stepped in. Tom could make out a man in a black robe and white collar, a priest, probably. He could remember priests. The priest's hair was a tall pile of black curls on top of his head, as if his hair were trying to get to heaven first. He could see Tom. He glanced at him, smiled, and looked again. Tom's stomach didn't seem to mind this man seeing him.

"I'm just waiting for Future Shop to open," Tom said.

"Ah." The man's voice was old, but his face was young. "Sit, then."

"I like to catch the morning news on one of the TVs," Tom said. "I like to stay current."

"You don't have a TV in your house?"

"Don't have a house," Tom said.

The priest pressed his fingertips together and nodded thoughtfully. He didn't stare at Tom, but he didn't make Tom invisible either.

"Are you Catholic?" the priest asked.

"I forget," Tom said. "I think so." He thought maybe his family was Catholic, or maybe Buddhist.

"One doesn't forget if one is Catholic," the priest said. "But we serve all God's children here. Rich or poor, it is all the same to God."

"You must have found Him, then."

"Who?"

"God."

"Oh." The man nodded, and so did his hair. He smiled. "It is not finding Him that is difficult, it is following Him that takes a lifetime. Are you hungry? I have some cookies in the office—"

"Do you talk to Him?" Tom asked.

The priest was silent for a time. "I do," he said finally.

"Maybe you could tell Him about me," Tom said. "Just in case He's forgotten."

"God does not forget His children."

Tom thought about the woman he had seen this morning sleeping on a park bench and wearing red high heels. She had such small feet.

"Well, just in case," Tom said. "Have you ever run into a boy named Daniel Wolflegs?"

"Daniel. Good name." He thought for a moment. "Tall?"

"I don't know," Tom said. He dug the school photo out of his pocket and showed the priest.

"Yes. I haven't seen him in a while, though. First time I met him, some kids were egging the church. He chased them off. I saw him eating the eggs they left. Raw. I talked to him for a while, learned his name, but when I suggested he go home, he bolted."

"Next time you see him, tell him Tom is looking for him. A nice guy. I'm always around." Tom began to leave, then turned and added, "And next time you're talking to God, maybe you could tell Him that if rich or poor's all the same to Him, I'd rather be rich."

"I'll do that," the priest said. "I believe, however, you should approach him about it yourself."

"Yeah. Well, Future Shop is open," he said, and he left.

A new clerk gave Tom a Mozart CD. "It's *The Magic Flute*," the clerk said.

"Hey, thanks," Tom said brightly because of nice.

He put the headphones on.

He listened.

The first strains were familiar, beautiful . . . but . . .

He tore off the headphones.

Gravity.

When he saw the clerk staring at him, he realized that he was gasping like he'd just run a mile. Tom could feel that morning's distressed green apples in his stomach creeping back up into his mouth. He ran out of Future Shop and threw up into an open waste bin in the parking lot.

He needed to hide. Gravity was looking at him, concentrating all its efforts on him. He went around to the back of the church and crawled under the skirt of a large pine tree. He lay there breathing deeply for a long time, and then he fell asleep.

The priest found him in the morning. He bent down on his knees, looked under the tree, and got up again. A little while later he was back. He rolled two bagels to Tom, rolled them like tires toward him. Tom ate them before he came out. When he did, the priest was watching for him.

"Can I use the bathroom?" Tom asked.

The priest showed him the way.

"Shower," he said, and he handed Tom a towel.

Showers, Tom decided, were one of the great inventions of mankind. In the shower, he knew that it wasn't Mozart's fault. He knew Mozart had won the hide-and-seek with God. He could tell that just by listening to his music for a minute. But there was gravity in it, serious gravity that squeezed out all your stomach contents. He thought he'd heard that music before, knew it in fact. Just those few bars made him see himself, dirty; made him smell himself. This was crazy, sleeping in a park like this. Why didn't he just go to the police and find his parents? Why didn't he do something, anything?

The priest invited him to sit in the chapel alone while he went about his work. Tom said, "Thank you." He still didn't feel very good. He remembered the feeling of gravity in the music. This is what gravity could do to you if it decided to pick on you: it made you too heavy to get up and look for a job; it made your heart so heavy inside that you could feel it beating where your stomach should be, and how could you care about anything with your heart half-eaten-up like that? It made breathing take all your energy. Sitting up deserved applause; making yourself clean deserved a hero's medal.

Tom was suddenly angry. He wasn't going to let it. He was going to look up; he was going to look it in the eyeball, gravity's heavy, round, slimy eyeball.

He opened his book.

Something had happened to Tom, but that was the first thing he forgot. Too bad, because Tom, he was a nice guy.

He wrote in the margin beside this entry: **Something bad, something to do with Mozart.**

He puzzled over this for a moment. He wasn't sure if he was writing fiction or not. It had to be true, or it wasn't anything. Beside **Tom found food,** he wrote **Tom is a garbage eater.** In the margin beside **Tom lives on Prince's Island,** he wrote **Tom evacuated in a public place.**

He could write **2 + 2 = 5** if he wanted, he knew that, but if he did, nothing would ever make any sense. You only had to listen to a minute of Mozart to realize you had to figure things out. He just didn't know what was true. He didn't remember what was true.

Later in the afternoon, the priest sat down near Tom. He held out two new twenty-dollar bills.

Tom hesitated.

"We are all beggars before God," the priest said, placing the money on the pew beside Tom.

Tom looked at his notebook. "I'm looking for a job. I'm saving to rent a billboard."

The priest said nothing for a moment. His hair shook a little.

He folded his hands as if they were just sitting together being quiet on purpose.

"I asked about Daniel Wolflegs for you," the priest said.

"You did?"

"Only one person I spoke with had seen him recently. He saw him . . ." He cleared his throat. "He saw him at a house where illegal substances can be purchased."

"Where?"

"I don't know the address. This person called it . . . 'The Eye.' That's all. The Eye."

Tom knew right away where it was. It was an old house with a huge eye painted on the side of it. Suddenly, he felt good. He felt clean, full of bagels, rich, and like he was going to find Daniel, and then home, and soon this would all be over.

"I guess you don't believe in magic," Tom said.

"What kind of magic?"

"A medicine man said I was a Finder."

The priest nodded. "Did you find anything?"

"A pen," Tom said.

The priest rubbed his beard and then folded his hands again.

"A magic pen," Tom said. "And a blanket and a bakery dumpster . . ."

The priest considered his folded hands.

"Seems like whatever I write comes true," Tom said.

The priest nodded, and after a time said, "This I do know: Words have the power to create and destroy, to wound and to heal. God created the world with words. One of His titles, in fact, is 'The Word'." He clasped and unclasped his hands. "Unfortunately, sometimes I am so busy with words that I forget that they cannot be eaten. Tom, will you let us help you? If you don't have a place to go, there are people who can help you."

"I'm sure I have a home. My parents just haven't found me yet," Tom said. "They might be rich so I can pay you back the money."

"No. Please." He stood up and put his hand on Tom's head. "I love you, my boy. Go to the police. Surely they will help you find your parents."

Tom said, *I love you, too,* but not out loud. Something inside him said it, something in the vicinity of his wishbone.

So, Tom thought, *that's where You are.*

Tom left to find The Eye. On the way he stopped and wrote in his book, **Tom found God.**

Tom had seen the house before in his wanderings, and he easily found it again. As he came closer he could see that the pupil of the eye was a black bird or a pterodactyl or something. Tom stood on the sidewalk and took a deep breath.

P–T–E–R–O–D–A–C–T–Y–L.

He smiled and marched to the door. Someone was playing drums inside. He knocked. A man with hair down to his waist answered the door.

"I was told I might find Daniel Wolflegs here," Tom said to him.

The man turned away and shouted, "There's a kid with a backpack here, looking for Daniel."

Tom didn't hear the answer over the drums, but the man turned back to him and said, "Not here."

"Do you know where—"

"Sorry."

Tom put his left hand up to the door frame just as the man shut it. Slam. Tom could hear little bones snap. The door bounced open.

Tom knew a trick.

He separated his mind from his body.

His hand had just been murdered, but that had nothing to do with him. With his brain he wondered how he had learned to do that, while the whole time his hand was screaming.

The man with the long hair stared at Tom as if he were the living dead. He was afraid of Tom. Tom decided this was a power almost as good as fighting.

"I need to know if Daniel is really here or not," Tom said. His voice hardly shook. "I have to talk to him." Don't move the hand, he told himself. Don't move the hand. It had turned a grayish color and was oozing blood.

The man shook the hair from his face. His mouth was open, and his eyes were open wide. Tom wanted to cradle his hand in his chest, but he didn't.

"No. He's really not here. And I'm going to close this door now, whether your hand is in the way or not."

Tom barely got his hand out of the way before the door slammed again.

Tom walked away, holding his hand upright against his chest.

The throbbing in his hand beat in time with his heart. He was all one piece now, his hand and his heart. His whole body hurt. He licked his hand as he walked. It cooled it.

It was getting dark, but he knew these streets like the back of his hand now, and they were both broken.

Chapter 4

I chattered—and that was bad.
— Act 2, scene 29

On the way back to the island, Tom sauntered back and forth in front of the police headquarters. For the first while he hoped someone would come running out, saying they had just got his picture and his parents were searching frantically for him and what was wrong with his poor hand. When that didn't happen, he hoped he'd get the guts to go in. Finally, he gave up, told himself he'd go in on a hungry day when there wasn't anything in his stomach to throw up.

As usual, Tom saw Samuel Wolflegs on the bench by the river.

He was getting used to the routine. "What did you find today, Tom Finder?" Samuel said to him as he came closer. "Never mind. Looks like you found a fight."

"Sort of," Tom said.

Samuel led him to the river and got him to put his hand in the water. It felt good. In a few minutes Samuel looked at it, made Tom move his wrist, his fingers.

"Hospital," Samuel said.

"No," Tom said.

Samuel didn't argue. "Not much they can do with hands anyway." He pulled an enormous handkerchief out of his pocket and wrapped Tom's hand up snugly. "So, what did you find today, Tom Finder?"

"Food" and "money" had been good enough the first few times he'd been asked to report. After that they had not been acceptable answers. Samuel Wolflegs liked to hear answers that told him Tom was looking, really looking. He would look at him with a wolf in his eyes which made the hair stand straight up on Tom's forearms and made Tom remember that this man knew where he slept. He had grown so thin that Tom didn't think he could hurt him much, but his wolf's eye had grown hungrier. His beautiful beaded jacket hung loose on him.

"I found that if you look in their eyes, people have signs just like streets," Tom said.

For a moment the wolf looked as if it would prefer to eat pizza rather than boy.

"Tell me," he said.

"Well, most people have 'yield' signs in their eyes: You may sit here as long as you don't sit too long. Security guards have yield signs. The priest at the cathedral on Seventh has a 'one way' sign. The train cops and the police have 'stop' signs: you can't sit here, you can't eat here. Then there's the do-gooders. Nice people, bring you tea and sandwiches, but their eyes have signs saying 'no exit.' And then there's some people who have 'danger' signs . . ."

Samuel nodded. "You are a Finder," he said, almost as if to comfort himself. "You know those danger signs, Tom, but watch out for those with 'dead end' eyes, too. They seem like friends at first, but you meet them at night in the dark. You cannot see that they only want to rob you, and not just of money."

Tom looked for the peach Samuel often had for him.

"What else did you find today, Tom?"

Maybe it wouldn't be a peach—maybe a cheese sandwich, or a chocolate bar. "God," Tom said. "I found God."

"Too easy," Wolflegs said. "What about my boy, Daniel?"

Tom shook his head. He'd heard so much about Daniel that he was beginning to miss him, too. He sighed.

"He has a scar on his chin, don't forget," Samuel said. "When you're looking . . . he has lots of scars. Didn't think he'd live to be the age of twelve, that boy." He chuckled. "He never walked—only ran. He never walked around things, he climbed over them. He has scars from climbing fences, trees, falling off bikes, horses, skateboards. Once when he was seven he found a bullet—decided to see what would happen if he hit it with a rock. He's got a hole in his shin from that one." Samuel shook his head and laughed a little, and then his mouth bent down and he pressed his thumbs into his eyes.

"Sorry," Tom said, because of nice.

"Being a Finder doesn't mean you find everything right away," Wolflegs said gently.

"Who did he hang with?" Tom asked. "Do you know the name of any of his friends?"

"Pepsi," Wolflegs said. "I remember Pepsi. I don't know his real name."

So Tom looked for Pepsi, who was much easier to find.

Tom found a tiny green park in the Core. When street people walked by, he asked them about a kid named Pepsi. You could tell the street people. They acted like the street was the place where they could sleep and eat and make out and cry and laugh as loud as they wanted.

Tom liked this park. It was just the size of a house lot between two skyscrapers, green, and carefully landscaped. There was a cement waterfall, flowers, a few bushes, a bench, and one enormous tree, which looked small, dwarfed between the towers on either side of the park.

Today, on the bench was a silver-haired man in a suit and tie and a black all-weather coat. His briefcase was the thinnest. He was sitting with his head tipped back to the sun, his eyes closed, his hands clasped behind his neck. From the saggy look of the old guy's face, Tom figured he must have fought and lost a few battles with gravity in his life.

Tom stared. He'd never seen a downtown worker sit on a bench, just doing nothing, just letting the sunshine fall on his face. The downtown workers usually didn't stop except at red lights, and sometimes not even then.

The man felt Tom's stare and opened his eyes. Tom wanted to ask, "Are you my dad?" Instead he said, "Are you rich?"

The man straightened his head. "You don't look much like a mugger," he said.

Tom shifted his backpack. "I'm not."

The man looked at Tom a long moment, closed his eyes, and raised his face to the sun again. "Yes. I suppose by some standards one could say I was rich."

"How'd you make your money? Don't say hard work, because you're just sitting."

The man chuckled. "You may have a point there. I made my money in the stock market. Company shares."

"The company shared?"

"Well, I had to have a little capital."

"What's capital?"

"Money."

Tom nodded. "Got me some capital in a locker at the Greyhound station."

"Well, son, my advice to you is to invest. By the time you're my age, you'll be a wealthy man."

"I can't wait that long," Tom said. "Have you got any more advice?"

The man shaded his eyes and looked at Tom. "Do what you love. If you love it, you'll do it well. If you do it well, the world will reward you. What do you love to do?"

"I like to write things." Tom glanced up at the sky, as if gravity were there waiting to pounce.

The man nodded. "That's along my line of work. I'm in newspapers." He handed Tom a card.

"Yeah? Maybe if I wrote something down, you'd pay me money for it."

The man eased back in the bench and raised his face to the sun. "That what you're doing it for? Money?"

"No. Maybe."

The man laughed shortly. "See, I could retire. I could have retired ten years ago. I don't because of words."

He opened one eye to see if Tom was listening. He was.

"I read a great book once," the old man said. "It was better than money. I realized having a word was more than having a buck."

Tom nodded slowly.

"Think of a word," the man said.

"Gravity," said Tom.

The old man pointed a long finger at him.

"Now there's a word. Gravity was here before there were words. But did we know that? Not until we named it did we really start to learn about it. Now, think of the word *antigravity*."

Tom shook his head. His neck and jaw creaked. "No such thing."

"No? But just because there's a word for it, every year millions in dollars and big brains go into looking for it. By gum, they'll find it, too."

Tom thought about antigravity. It was like mooning the universe to even say it.

"If I wrote something, would you tell me if the world would reward me for it?" Tom asked.

"You can find me here early mornings. Got osteoporosis—a woman's disease. I don't tell anybody but you. I need my vitamin D."

"My name's Tom."

The man peered at him with an eye that could assess. "You're not in school?"

"I don't have a school."

"Ah. You have a home?"

"No. At least, temporarily no." T–E–M–P–O–R–A–R–I–L–Y.

"What's it like living on the streets?" the man asked.

Tom was going to explain that he wasn't living on the streets, he was living on an island, but the man spoke again.

"Why don't you write it down for me, what it's like to be living here on the streets, how you got there—"

"I'm not really—"

"I'd pay for that," the man said. "Good money for that. If you can write, of course." The man stood, picked up his thin briefcase. "Back to work." He nodded curtly to Tom and left.

He wasn't a street kid. He was an island kid. He was between addresses, a temporarily lost soul.

Tom walked past the cement waterfall and noticed that people had thrown change into it as if it were a wishing well. He determined to come back later that night and collect the change.

When it got dark, Tom returned to the park. It had been a hot day, so he bathed in the waterfall and the pool below it before he collected the change. He sat under a tree to count it. The tree rustled without wind.

"You stealin' wishes, man," a voice said above him.

Tom jumped to his feet.

It sounded as if it were coming from the sky, and for a moment Tom wondered if God was speaking to him. He looked up. He could see a small platform lodged in the crotch of the branches, and leaning out from the platform was a black head.

"Who is it?"

"Don't believe you, man. You stealin' people's wishes they made. Might have to fight you for that."

"They wished a kid could have his wish today," Tom said. "I'm just making sure their wish comes true."

"Well, I got twelve dollars worth of wishes in there, and I jus' as poor as you." Tom thought a minute. He dropped the coins back into the water.

The black head flashed two rows of the whitest teeth Tom had ever seen, and then Tom recognized the face. "Hey, you're the one who helped me get away from the Train Cop."

"Come up. I got sunflower seeds, the kind with dried worms in the bottom of the bag."

Tom climbed. He was nervous. Climbing made you vulnerable to gravity's tricks, especially when you had a sore hand. The platform was covered in down coats.

"You sleep here at night?" Tom asked.

The black kid nodded. "Can't stand walls. Name is Jeans."

"Tom."

"After the train I seen you in the park a few times. Been tryin' to figure you out. Maybe you a Head?"

"What's that?"

"If you don't know what it means, then you not it. Well, you don't belong to my gang, so what are you?"

Tom hesitated a moment. No one knew what a Finder was, and he didn't feel like getting into that discussion. He said, "I'm a writer."

Jeans's teeth flashed like a crescent moon. "Maybe you like to join my gang."

"Gang?"

"Yeah. The Perfs. You gotta have a hole in you to join. Ever been shot or stabbed?"

"No."

"Well, maybe you tell them you a writer and they'll let you join 'cause of the hole in your head." Jeans laughed and then stopped. "Just a joke, man. Here, have some sunflower seeds."

Tom took a huge handful.

"I seen you runnin' from the train cops," Jeans said. "You a sweet nanny goat jus' runnin' its belly. Why don't you jus' buy a ticket?"

"Can't," said Tom with a mouthful of sunflower seeds.

"Can't?"

"Mean to. Mean to every time. But I'm savin'."

"Saving? Saving for what?"

"Savin' to be rich."

"Me too," Jeans said.

Tom wanted to smile, but his cheek muscles still hadn't remembered how. "What are you getting rich to buy?"

"Gonna buy me a ticket back to Jamaica. Got me a girl there name of Gina, and she waitin' on me." Jeans settled down into the nest of coats. A few feathers floated up.

"Port Antonio is where she is, my girl Gina. I met her there while working as a chicken cooker. That's how I got a hole in me—dropped a knife on my foot—but don't tell Sasky that. I save my money, and I have just enough to buy her a gold weddin' band. Then I begin to be thinkin' about how I could buy a plane ticket with that money, how I should come to visit cousin Walter in Canada and make so much money. Gina, she says to buy that plane ticket, that be my ring. I say, no, that is your ring and your house and your microwave oven, don't you see?"

"But I didn't count on all the walls makin' me crazy. Chicken cookers work inside here. Almost go zoid in all those walls. But I gotta get back. Gina, she said she kill me twice, once for fun and once for sure, if I don't be true to her. She gonna think I run off for good. She gonna marry somebody else, and that would kill me all by itself."

"Anyone that mean is still waiting for you," Tom said, trying to comfort him.

Jeans rolled in the coats. "You think?"

"Sure," Tom said.

"You got a way with words, man," Jeans said. "Maybe you a writer after all."

Tom ate the seeds from the top of the bag. "I'm looking for a job for now. A real job."

Jeans laughed. "Nobody gonna give you a job."

"Why not?"

" 'Cause, don't you see, you a street kid! What can you do?"

Tom shrugged. "I can swim. And spell."

"You got a diploma? References? What your SIN? Hell's bells, you don't even have a address or a shower. You are what they call *un-stay-bull*."

Tom spat out some shells. "If you're so smart, you tell me how to get rich."

Jeans leaned back into the coats. "You gotta get a university education."

"Yeah? How do you do that?"

"Easy. You fill out forms, you pay tuition."

"Tuition?"

"Money."

"Got some tuition in a locker at the Greyhound," Tom said. "So, why don't you get a university education?"

"First I gotta get home and get my girl, Gina. I need a job."

"But you're a street kid, too."

"Yeah, but I got somethin' that's gonna make them forget that: posture."

Tom gaped at him a moment. "Posture?"

"Posture. You just look at them downtown folks. They all stand so straight and tall. You hunch over all the time, half in your pockets. Easy to tell you street-lovin'."

Tom thought about it a moment, then nodded. "I'll try it," he said. "Well, I guess I've got to go." Tom began to climb down from the tree.

"Hey, whatcha gettin' rich to buy?"

"A billboard," Tom said. "I only need $5,326 now." He was trying to keep his back straight as he climbed down.

Jeans started to laugh. He laughed the whole time Tom was climbing down. When Tom touched ground and looked up, he could see feathers from holes in the down coats flying like snow.

"You a writer for sure, man," Jeans called down. "Nothin' you say make sense." Tom could see Jeans's head, a spoon of a head only a little blacker than the night sky, leaning out from the platform.

"Well, I forgot to tell you. I'm not just a writer. I'm a Finder."

"What's a finder?"

"I find things."

"Like what?"

"Like jobs. And money, and muffins. And other stuff."

"How you get to be like that?"

"A medicine man told me I had the gift."

"Sheesh. Whatever. You let me know if you find a job with no walls, Mr. Finder," Jeans said.

"Sure," Tom said. "By the way, do you know a kid named Pepsi?"

"I do. He hang in the Devonian garden. He is there, but he not easy to find. 'Cept for you, maybe, huh?"

Jeans's moon smile floated a moment in the spoon sky and was gone. Rolling his pen between his fingers, Tom walked to his island.

Tom found out that the Devonian garden was a huge indoor jungle. The downtown workers ate their lovely-looking lunches there. He went there the next evening.

He didn't know how anybody could hang out there. It was humid in the atrium jungle, and Venus gravity. He felt as if he were in an aquarium and any minute someone would reach in with a giant net and pluck him out. He hung out all evening, and he went back again the next day. That night he stayed until the last person left before lockup for the night. He hid under a huge umbrella plant until the lights dimmed and the footsteps of the security guard faded away. He and Pepsi both emerged from hiding at the same time.

Pepsi was about his age, with his hair in a ponytail hanging out the back of his baseball cap. His hair was pink, and the shadows under his eyes were almost black. His lips were gray, and his eyes bloodshot red. His colors were in all the wrong places.

"Pepsi?"

"Who's asking?"

"Tom." He held out his hand. Well-mannered, that's what he was. He'd have to write that down. Pepsi ignored his hand and began picking at his neck, which was covered in sores. "I'm looking for a guy named Daniel. Daniel Wolflegs. I need to talk to him. Someone told me you might know where he was."

Pepsi considered him for a minute. "I heard you were asking

for Daniel. I was thinking you look like a burb kid, and I'm wondering why a burb kid would be looking for Daniel."

"Burb kid?"

"Burb kids come to the streets because they think the world is only as bad as their daddy. Come to think of it, you've been here too long to be a burb kid. Maybe you're a freep. Are you a freep?"

Tom stared at him.

"Freep. Kids who come to streets a bit at a time, going to the bars and the pool halls, parties, couch-surfing. Then hard people start putting the pressure on them to earn their keep." He smiled. "That was me."

"I'm looking for a job," Tom said.

Pepsi laughed. "You're a funny man." He took a half-smoked cigarette out of his pocket and stuck it in his mouth. He looked at Tom. "How old are you?"

"Um . . . about sixteen," Tom said.

Pepsi sucked on the unlit cigarette. "More like fourteen. Did you know that there are only two words in the English language that end in *g–r–y*?"

Tom shook his head.

"Hungry and angry," Pepsi said. Tom waited for him to light the cigarette, but he didn't. "How come you never smile?" Pepsi asked.

"My brain smiles," Tom said. "It's just that my face isn't attached to my brain anymore."

Pepsi walked around him, and Tom kept turning to face him. "So. Everyone's here for a reason. You've got your punch kids, and your diddle kids. Those ones are the runaways. Then you've got your throwaways."

"I just want to know where I can find Daniel Wolflegs. I heard you were his friend."

Pepsi sucked on the unlit cigarette again as if it were a soother. "As I was saying about throwaways . . . Daniel is a throwaway. His dad said he could do his drugs somewhere not in his house. They changed the locks on him." Pepsi laughed low, then rubbed his eyes. "So, what are you?"

"What am I?"

Pepsi just looked at him hard with his red eyes.

"I'm a Finder." Tom didn't know why he said it. Maybe just to hear Pepsi laugh. It worked. It made his face go from old to fifteen.

"What's a Finder?" Pepsi said, still laughing. "Some kind of superhero?"

"They find things."

"Like what?"

"Like what they're looking for. It . . . it's a gift. Daniel's dad, Samuel Wolflegs, told me I had the gift."

"You're messing with me."

"So have you seen Daniel around?"

Pepsi came right up to Tom. "You're zoid," he said.

"What's that?"

Pepsi shoved his face into Tom's. Tom wasn't scared. He must have been able to fight before the Forgetting. Yeah, he was pretty sure he could remember what if felt like to get punched in the face. He had to write that down, that he could fight. Besides, Pepsi seemed thin and weak. Tom could take him.

"Tough, huh?" Pepsi said. He grinned and backed up a step. He shrugged. "Can't hurt me anyway since I'm already dead."

Tom remembered the old man under the bridge. "Dead?"

"Cracked head," Pepsi said, pointing to the top of his head. He laughed at the expression on Tom's face. "It's Forget. You know? People say it's killing me, but I say that happened a long time ago." Pepsi came close to him, but this time it was to put his arm around him. He spoke to him in a confiding voice.

"See, Tom, when someone takes their first crack at it, that's when they decide to die. They get high as heaven, but they can't stay there. They keep coming down to dead, and every time they come down they're deader than before. They try again, but heaven won't keep them, and people keep charging them for a peek. Pretty soon they just want to be dead even if it means hell. One day they find out they're so dead that the worms are eating them up, coming right out of the pores of their skin. They pick at them, and that's what gives them sores, all that picking at worms."

"There's no worms," Tom said, looking at Pepsi's neck.

"You can tell them that. They might even believe you. But they still pick." Pepsi flicked Tom's cheek. "I tell you that so you'll know. Forget means die."

Pepsi began walking away as if the conversation was over.

"Hey," Tom said. "Hey! Please, just tell me where to find Daniel. Look, I promise, I don't want anything bad to happen to him. If he tells me to leave him alone, I will. Where could I find him?"

"I forget," Pepsi said, and he laughed. But in a moment he said, "Look, I don't know where he is. He's sick, you know? But you might try Jon Jonson's. Jon's a consumer, a real criminal element. Rents the Head house."

Tom wanted to ask what the "head house" was, but Pepsi didn't stop talking long enough to ask. "Very uptight guy, has some sort of reputation to uphold. He golfs, man, if you can believe it. You could try the youth shelter, too. Daniel goes there sometimes when he doesn't feel up to things."

"Thanks," Tom said.

Pepsi nodded. He butted the still-unlit cigarette on a bench and pocketed it again. He glanced at Tom as if he might have more to say, then walked away without looking back.

Tom walked the other direction to the doors of the Devonian. He knocked ten minutes before a security guard came to let him out.

It took Tom a day and a few more blisters to find the Head house. He knew it when he'd found it. It had a large wooden fence. One of the wooden gatepost tops had been carved into the head of an old man.

Tom's hand had been feeling better, but it throbbed once as he opened the gate. He held it up to his chest again.

The lawn was trim, and the house had been painted a conservative gray with dark charcoal trim. Tall lilies grew by the porch. No one walking by would notice this house if it weren't for the carved head on the gatepost. When Tom knocked, no one came to the door. He could hear music. After knocking a third time, he opened the door. There was hardwood flooring and a plant in a large pot in the hallway. Tom licked his hand, took a deep breath, and walked in. In the living room to his right, several people were splayed out on a couch and on the rug. One man with a short, neat haircut lifted his head from the back of the couch. He regarded Tom with calm eyes.

"If you're a narc, you're too late. It's all gone," he said. He let his head fall back onto the couch.

"I'm looking for Daniel Wolflegs," Tom said. He was searching for Daniel while he said it, but Daniel wasn't there.

The man asked a girl beside him, "If a thief walks into my house, doesn't that give me the right to shoot him or something?"

Tom felt something beating in his chest area, but he couldn't tell if it was his hand or his heart. "I'm just looking for Daniel Wolflegs," he said. "Pepsi told me I might find him here."

The man didn't raise his head again. He said, "And I'm looking for a reason to shoot you. Asking for Daniel is good enough."

"It's just a kid," the girl beside him on the couch drawled. "Daniel isn't here, kid," she said to Tom. "He hasn't been here for a long time. You'd better go."

Tom and his hand were both glad to get out of there.

Tom found the youth shelter next.

A social worker with bright red hair told him that Daniel stayed there sometimes, but no one had seen him for a few weeks. She invited Tom to stay there that night. She gave him toothpaste.

The shelter smelled of cigarette smoke so strongly that you couldn't smell any other smell. A few kids were watching TV in the living room. They only glanced at him, but they did see him. *One of us*, their eyes said. It made Tom uneasy. He didn't like the way others saw him. He wasn't one of them. He wanted to make himself up. Tom went upstairs to a bed, sat on the edge, and took out his book and pen.

He opened his book. Remembering that he hadn't backed down from Pepsi, and sure of the memory of getting punched in the face, he wrote: **Tom Finder can fight.**

He was making himself up, inventing the story of himself. You could do that when you didn't know anything about yourself, when you'd forgotten everything. When you had only a few days of yourself to remember, you could write down everything you knew about yourself.

He closed the book, then opened it again. He wrote: **He is a man**—yes, he liked that—**who keeps a promise. He will find Daniel Wolflegs before he goes home.** That was good writing.

Tom lay on the springy mattress, which smelled of tobacco smoke and throw-up. He got his pen ready in case he thought up a nice design for the billboard.

Wanted: Parents of Tom. Then what? He didn't have a phone number. Maybe this: **Lost son? Check Prince's Island Park.** No. Too many words. Besides, that could be any number of boys. It had to be catchy and bold. His dad might be an advertising executive. He'd expect Tom to display some creativity.

While he was thinking about it, a girl sat beside him.

"You're the poet," she said.

Tom stared.

"We've seen you around, writing in that book. We call you the poet. What are you writing now?" she asked.

Tom closed the book. "Nothing."

"Cool. That's what I write, too," the girl said. She looked overweight and malnourished at the same time, as if she ate only potato chips. Tom realized he had seen the girl before, standing on the street corner near the day care. Her hair hadn't been washed in a while, and there was dust and lint stuck to it. She had pretty eyes, but there was something spooky about them. She wasn't looking at his face or his haircut or his clothes or his crooked bottom tooth. She was looking at the backs of his eyes.

Tom looked away.

"I'm Janice. What's your name?"

Tom didn't think he could look back into her eyes, even knowing about nice.

"Hey. Aren't you going to answer her?" In the doorway stood another girl. She was the most beautiful real live girl he had ever seen. She was wearing a tight T-shirt that said CANADIAN GIRLS KICK ASS. He wished someone would kick his so he could stop reading her T-shirt.

Tom swallowed and looked into the other girl's spooky eyes. "I'm Tom."

"The poet," Janice said.

"Well, I just write things—not poetry, but—"

"Oh," Janice said. She stood up. "Well, I only talk to poets."

"Why?"

Janice looked at him and turned away without answering. Tom saw the Canadian girl smile. She was going to leave with her. "Hey," he said quickly. "Do you know a kid named Daniel Wolflegs?"

T-shirt girl shook her head, but Janice nodded.

"I need to talk to him. Can you tell me where to find him?"

"Sorry," Janice mouthed, with no sound. "I only talk to poets."

The T-shirt girl shrugged and smiled at him and began to turn away.

"What if I was a Finder?"

They stopped.

"What's a finder?" the poet asked the T-shirt girl.

"What's a finder?" the T-shirt girl asked Tom.

How could he think when the words on her T-shirt expanded and shrunk like that when she spoke?

"Uh . . . it might be a kind of poet," he finally thought to say. Anything to make that girl stay.

Poet girl looked at him skeptically. "Okay, read me one of your poems," she said without sound.

"She says, read her one of your poems," T-shirt girl said.

Tom squirmed uncomfortably. He opened his book so that only he could see the words. He could make it up on the spot, but what if she really was a poet and she could tell? He decided to read her something he had written in his book.

It might have something to do with drums.
I remember drums.
The other music is gone.
I remember fighting.
And gravity. That gravity always wins.
Without it we would all fly off into space, and the
earth would wander, and the whole universe would close
up like a book. With it, we can't fly, and we always lose.
I remember that, too.

When he was done, T-shirt girl looked questioningly at Janice.

Janice shrugged. "Good try," she said out loud. T-shirt girl smiled, a big smile, the most perfectly beautiful Canadian smile Tom had ever seen. It was obvious to him now that the way to get to know this girl was to be nice to her poet friend. Luckily for him, nice came easy.

"Read me one of your poems," he said to the poet girl.

Poet girl looked uncomfortably at Tom, and then at the T-shirt girl. T-shirt girl frowned and put her arm around poet girl. "You can't read her poetry."

"Why?" Tom asked.

"Because," she answered. "Because it's all space. People never stop to think that it's the spaces inside the letters that make the letters. Letters are just spaces on a string. Everyone thinks the lines are so great, nobody thinks about the space. Janice celebrates space."

Janice the poet girl smiled at T-shirt girl. "Yes," she said. "That's it."

Tom thought there must be a lot of space inside Janice's head, but he only nodded.

Janice smiled at Tom. She hadn't brushed her teeth in a while. "Hey," she said. "I liked the way you answered: with space. You didn't say anything."

"What's your name?" Tom asked T-shirt girl.

"Pam. Yours?"

"Tom. So you must write poetry, too, since Janice talks to you."

"Nope. No poetry in me. I tell futures," Pam said.

"That are sheer poetry," Janice said.

"So how come you're here?" Tom asked, nodding at the walls of the shelter.

Pam shrugged. "Just for a while, until I get a job. I'm going to be a window dresser. I've applied at a few places. They say come back when I'm done high school. Like anything I'd learn in high school has anything to do with being a window dresser."

"I'm looking for my daughter," Janice said. Tears spurted from her eyes, completely missing the tops of her cheeks and splashing halfway down. She blinked in surprise, as if someone had thrown water into her face.

Pam put her arm around the other girl. "C'mon, Janice. Let's get some sleep."

"Listen," Janice said to Tom. "Daniel hangs with the dead. I don't know his people. But you might try hanging out at the LRT station. I've seen him there. He's been sick, strung out. Bring some smokes for bait. Got to go. I need my space."

After they left Tom wrote in his book, **Tom found a girl.** He closed the book, then opened it again. **Tom is a poet,** he wrote. **A Canadian poet.**

Chapter 5

You go on blowing your flute, I am going to play a different tune.
                                                    – Act 2, scene 28

That night Tom was awakened often, every time the toilet flushed, every time someone cried out in his sleep. Someone was snoring. A few people were laughing all night long. They were going to sleep when Tom got up. It was still dark out, and the social worker was sleeping. Tom took a shower, ate some cornflakes, brushed his teeth with the toothpaste, and left. It felt good to be clean, but the shelter made him uneasy. The red-haired social worker looked at him a lot and asked him hard questions like, "What's your last name?"

When his parents looked at him, the day they found him, they would see him the way he really was: nice, good speller, able to hold his own in a fight. A God-fearing swimmer. And a saver. Maybe he'd gotten that from his mom. His dad was probably the kind that spent too much money on stuff for his son. They were probably worried sick, calling all his friends, the police.

Why didn't he just go to the police?

No.

Something to do with gravity. Something to do with the way he wanted to throw up and cry every time he even thought of it. His parents would understand when he told them about losing his memory, about needing to be invisible for a while. Tom went to the LRT station to look for Daniel.

The Stampede station was empty when he arrived. The smells of tobacco and perfume and fries hung in pockets that you could walk in and out of. The wind skittered cigarette butts and discarded tickets along the cement platform. He walked around the station while the sun lightened the sky. No one showed up that could be Daniel Wolflegs. Tom looked for good cigarettes to use as bait.

That day he found a lipstick, Tender Pink. He kept it all day. His eyes liked to lick it. He kept the lipstick in his pocket when he left the station to look for HELP WANTED signs. When he inquired, people were looking for someone older, or more experienced, or with a résumé.

You were allowed four nights in the shelter, so Tom slept there again. Janice the poet and Pam the Canadian weren't there. Tom showered and used mouthwash and stole three containers of floss.

The next morning he met up with the newspaper man again. This time his tie was off and his shirt collar unbuttoned and his sleeves rolled up.

"Well, it's the little mugger. Written anything for me yet?"

"Not for you. Just for me," Tom said.

"Yes? Let me look at it."

Tom hesitated, but the man gestured impatiently. He handed him his notebook.

The man read. Once he nodded. Twice he nodded. He handed it back to Tom.

"So?"

"Shows you can spell," the old man said.

"I can spell," Tom said.

"Spell *proficient*."

"P–R–O–F–I–C–I–E–N–T."

The man nodded. He unfolded a piece of tinfoil and held it under his chin.

"Am I a poet?" Tom asked.

"A poet? That's not my area of expertise. But I memorized a poem once in school. I can't remember the periodic table or the dates of a single war or how to multiply fractions, but I remember that poem." He closed his eyes and recited:

"Not in entire forgetfulness,
And not in utter nakedness,
But trailing clouds of glory do we come
From God, who is our home:
Heaven lies about us in our infancy!
Shades of the prison-house begin to close
Upon the growing Boy . . ."

His eyes popped open, and he eyed Tom. Perhaps he'd had second thoughts about Tom who-might-be-a-mugger.

"By William Wordsworth," he said. He looked at Tom for a long moment, then dismissed him with a gesture. "Go write something for me."

The next day, in the train station, he found an address book. He wondered what it would be like to have so many friends that you couldn't remember where they were. Or maybe the person just wrote them down so she could flip through the pages and feel lucky.

That night in the shelter a kid with a Betty Boop tattoo on his arm saw Tom's lipstick and told the supervisor that Tom wasn't a boy. Tom left, and threw the lipstick away on his way out.

The day after that Tom found a grocery list. At first he thought it was a poem in a foreign language, until he got to a part of the list he recognized as food: chicken, tomatoes, onions. But what were cumin, pesto, hoisin, and gingerroot? He wrote the strange words in his notebook so he wouldn't forget.

He felt like an archeologist trying to decipher the garbage of a lost people. The whole world seemed to understand something that Tom was trying to figure out. That was the worst thing about forgetting. The best thing was that anyone could be his mom. When people got off the trains, he picked the prettiest woman or the rich-looking one or the one with lots of kids, to imagine that she was his mother. He tried to catch the eye of the ones that looked smart. Proof that his mother was smart: he could spell. None of them saw him. He figured he wouldn't be invisible to his own mother.

Tom tried different LRT stations, looking for Daniel. When he found good cigarettes, he saved them, put them beside him on the bench. Only white kids tried to bum them. Sometimes he gave them out and said, "If you see a guy named Daniel Wolflegs, tell him I have to talk to him about something."

When the office-worker people were gone home and the station was empty except for the ghosts of smells, Tom would look for things and find them. Someone lost a book called *How to Improve Your Memory*. Tom read it cover to cover, but it didn't help.

The best thing he found was an entire purse. He studied it for hours before he turned it in. The wallet was stuffed with business cards, credit cards—one with the hologram of an eagle—and plastic-covered photos. There was a makeup case, a bag of lemon drops (Tom ate four), and a daytimer. The daytimer was full of the ordinary secrets of a good and invisible life, the life of someone that might have been his mother. He resolved that, being from an honest family, he would turn it in, though minus the $8.51 in the wallet which he would keep as a reward.

He decided to leave the purse on the doorstep of the police station. He walked back and forth on the street across from the station. Once, twice, three times. Every time he went to do it, he felt his bones go weak. Stepping off the curb to cross the street made him feel like he was going to fall. He told himself he would do it on the seventh try. Maybe seven had been his lucky number. The seventh time he told himself all the reasons why he could do it, why he could do anything he put his mind to. He was strong, up for a fight, able to swim and spell. On the seventh try he crossed the street halfway, chucked the purse at the steps, and ran.

He found a trash can in an alley and threw up the four lemon drops. Then he went to his locker at the Greyhound station and deposited eight dollars. He kept fifty-one cents for spending money.

Tom had been hanging out at LRT stations for over a week when the space poet showed up.

"Hey," she said, sitting down beside him. "Any luck finding Daniel?"

Tom shook his head. "How's the poetry?"

"That depends," she said.

"On what?"

"On what color the paper is."

She laughed. Tom cleared his throat. "So. Where's Pam?"

"New boyfriend."

"Oh." Tom looked down at the pile of cigarettes, thought maybe he should take up smoking, and then decided his parents were probably health-conscious and wouldn't approve.

"I came to tell you. She likes you. I bet you could get her away from him."

Tom shrugged. "Hey, it's her life. I don't even know her."

She didn't seem to hear him. "He's not a real boyfriend. He's a player, a seller. Used to hang out sometimes with my old boyfriend."

Tom sat up straight. "Well, why does she—?"

"She doesn't know. The guy comes along—Cupid, you'd think the name would tell her something. He buys her some clothes, takes her out to a real restaurant for dinner, tells her she's gorgeous, special. She thinks he loves her, thinks he's gonna take care of her, buy her a duplex and a dog. She wants a fence with sweet peas growing on it. He says: Sure, baby, sure, me too." Janice folded her arms over her chest. "Same old, same old."

"Didn't you tell her?"

"I did. She says I've gone zoid. She doesn't believe me. But you watch. In a couple of months he's gonna say: Baby, money is so bad right now and can you just do this one favor for me and then we'll be fine and we'll make our dreams come true and we'll go to TO and have a good time. Just a couple of weeks. If you really love me, you will."

"How do you know?"

" 'Cause that's the way it went for me. I got out of the life when my daughter was born." She was quiet a moment. She was looking into his eyes, even though he wasn't looking back. "You're not one of us," she said soberly.

He looked away.

"Pam says yes you are, but I say no, you are not one of us, not yet." She laughed and hit his arm. "But that's a good thing, right? Listen, are you really a Finder, Tom? Because if you are, could you look for my daughter? She looks like me, only cute."

"You really have a daughter?" Tom asked. "How old are you anyway?" Her spooky eyes stopped looking into the backs of his eyes and started looking into the backs of her own eyes.

Her voice seemed to come from her stomach. "I was the baby mom. My social worker took her away from me. You want what's best for her, don't you, she said. She said my baby's father was fishy. Fishy. So I said, well, we'll go away to the sea." Janice laughed too loudly. "I wanted to keep her, but they told me I shouldn't, if I loved her I wouldn't . . ." She rocked herself.

"Come on," Tom said. "I'll take you back to the shelter."

She got to her feet and walked beside him. She started hitting her left elbow with her right hand. She kept looking around, search-ing, as if she might see her daughter right there in the station.

"I told them I'd be good, I'd prove it to them, and then I'd come back for her. Now I'm being good. I just have to get a job or something. In the meantime, I look for her all the time, at all the babies I see, but none of them have fins." She laughed again. "Let's go to the park and look."

"Janice, come on. I'm taking you back to the shelter."

"Why?"

"Because."

"Why do people always say because?"

"Because."

She laughed and followed him. "My social worker said no guy who loves you would turn you out." She was quiet for a minute.

"It's good you got away from him," Tom said.

They walked a long time in silence. Once she said, "Anyway, just thought I'd tell you about Pam. Maybe you could talk to her." It was getting dark out. She sighed. "I'll tell you a secret, Tom. I saw my man once. In the river. I was standing on the bridge. He was underneath the water, staring up at me, asking me to jump to him. Jump, he said. The water's fine. Jump. I would have, if I hadn't remembered that I had to find my baby."

They had arrived at the shelter.

The red-haired social worker opened the door. She touched Janice's arm as she walked in. To Tom she said, "Coming in?"

Tom shook his head.

"Tom, who are you?"

"That's what I'm trying to find out," Tom said, and he said good-bye.

At the LRT station the wind blew over the platform. He sat heavily down on the bench and considered looking for Pam. He thought about her with Cupid and fought off an urge to break a window.

Maybe he had enough to look for. Daniel. His parents. A job. He picked up an old newspaper that had blown into a corner and turned to the personals section to see if anyone was looking for a boy named Tom. He'd picked up the obituary page. There was a picture of a young man, maybe sixteen, who looked familiar. Tom grabbed the paper with both fists to read it. *Sivorak, Peter.*

That name didn't sound familiar. He looked at the picture again. He knew that face. Maybe he'd known him in school. Maybe he could find these Sivorak people, say sorry about your boy, and do you know who I am? He read on.

Peter died after a long struggle with substance abuse. He is survived by his loving parents . . .

Substance abuse. Tom looked at the picture again, and then he knew who it was.

"Pepsi," he said aloud.

The train pulled in, silent on the rails, but Tom didn't pay attention. Gravity was trying to force him to put the paper down, but Tom wouldn't. He kept reading: *Peter was an avid Scouter as a youngster, and loved hockey . . .*

The train whispered to him as it pulled out. Tom looked up. He looked up just in time to see a warrior leaving the train platform. He was tall, wide-shouldered, and lean as a lost dog. His hair was long but not braided.

"Hey!" Tom shouted.

"Hey!" the station echoed back.

Hey, hey, hey . . .

Except it wasn't his own echo, it was Train Cop yelling. He was walking toward Tom, yelling something about not being on the platform without a ticket and something about a seven-hundred-dollar fine, something about lazy, smelly, snotty kids. Tom ran, still clutching the obituary column.

The tall boy had disappeared. Tom kept running. Finally, he stopped under a streetlight and read the obituary again. Could you get so invisible you disappeared from life? Stay away from Forget, Pepsi had warned him. Once you forget, you're already dead.

Tom walked until he was across from police headquarters. This could all be over so quick. Stupid to save for a billboard. Zoid, when you could just walk into a police station.

Gravity.

Needing-Gravol-type gravity.

Tom took a deep breath. He could do it. Anyone who could fight and write and swim could walk into a police station. Maybe his dad was a cop. Maybe his mom was a cop. That'd be just like her, to go and do something risky like that.

He walked in, clutching the obituary, his skin crawling, but it was all right, all right, because no one looked at him.

He stood a long time at the desk, holding onto it for fear he was going to fall. He gasped, startled, when an officer finally noticed him.

"What can I do for you?" the officer said without coming close to the desk. He put his hand on his hip, which was hung with a holster.

"Is anyone looking for me?" Tom asked. He was breathing hard, like he'd just run a long way, and the knuckles on his hand were white where he gripped the counter top. "Maybe someone rich?"

"Why? Are you lost?"

"I was just wondering if anyone called in looking for me."

"What's your name?"

"Tom."

"Tom what?"

"I don't know."

The officer studied him a minute, his fingers hooked on his gun belt. He went to a file on a desk. "I went through missing persons just this morning. I don't remember seeing a picture of you, but I'll check again." He shuffled through papers for a long time, occasionally glancing up at Tom. *Soon it would be over,* Tom thought. *Not so bad. Not so bad.* He was doing this. He'd sleep in his own bed tonight.

The officer said, "Nope."

Tom suddenly couldn't remember what that word meant.

"No one matching your description, kid, and no pictures of you."

Tom rocked on his feet. His neck shot with pain, as if gravity had just sat on his head. He felt his spine compress. He couldn't speak, couldn't say, "That can't be right."

"Listen, kid, I think you'd better come have a seat. Maybe we can help you."

Tom reached into his backpack and took out his book.

"What have you got there?" the officer asked.

Tom read his notes. Someone had thought he was nice. Nice didn't come from parents that didn't look for you. There had to be some kind of explanation. For a moment he thought about trusting the officer. Maybe he could help.

Tom took a deep breath and asked, "Can you tell me what happened to that dog that was hit on Macleod and Seventh?"

"Sure, I heard about that . . . Oh, so you're the one . . . Yeah, I heard about that."

"Where's the dog?"

"Put it out of its misery."

"They couldn't fix him?"

The officer shrugged. "Would have cost a fortune in vet fees. The system isn't set up to take care of strays."

Tom nodded slowly. "Makes sense," he said. He turned to walk out the door.

"Hey, where are you going? Maybe if I had a last name . . . You know your own last name, don't you, kid?" the officer called after him.

Tom walked until he was back to his island. Along the way he found a twenty-dollar bill. When he reached the island, Tom got out his notebook and wrote in it, **The streets love Tom.** He curled up in his blanket, and in the last fading light he read once more Peter Pepsi Sivorak's obituary.

He stared at the page a long time until all he could see was the space, the loopy letters, zeroes on a string.

Chapter 6

The streets loved him, but gave him only a little money at a time — mostly loonies and toonies and quarters, sometimes a five or a ten. He knew that at this rate he couldn't find enough money in a lifetime to rent a billboard. He couldn't think of what else to do. For a long time he thought about why his parents weren't looking for him. He figured they thought he'd run away over some typical teenage squabble and they were giving him his space. Maybe they thought he was visiting a relative. He probably had dozens of cousins, and an uncle who took him swimming.

He was looking for HELP WANTED signs and thinking of all this one morning when he walked into a bucket filled with water.

Someone snarled at him. "Hey, watch where you're going, or you'll kick the bucket all right."

It was the kid from the shelter with the Betty Boop tattoo on his arm. He was wearing a T-shirt with the sleeves ripped off, and Tom could see that he had a lot of other tattoos as well.

"Hey, it's the lipstick licker. What are you doing here, girl?"

"Looking for a job," Tom said. His legs twitched, ready to run.

"Yeah? Well, you're in my territory."

Tom glanced around. "It looks like a regular street to me." He told his legs to be still. He could fight if he had to, he reminded them.

Tom thought Betty Boop jiggled a bit. "Well, maybe you're not a girl after all, eh?" He pointed at himself. "Jamie."

"Tom."

Jamie spat. It lay there looking alive on the sidewalk. "Now, Tom, I'll explain to you. See, I'm a businessman. I provide a service—I clean windshields." He gestured toward the bucket Tom had kicked. It had two squeegees in it. "This is my corner. All the cars that come here are mine."

A businessman. That sounded good. His dad was probably one of those.

"How do I get a corner?" Tom asked.

"You got a work ethic?"

Tom thought he could probably find one.

" 'Cause you gotta hustle, you know. You gotta love customer service."

Tom nodded seriously.

Jamie sized him up. "I could probably arrange something for you. But first you've got to get yourself a little investment capital."

"I've got capital," Tom said.

"Yeah? How much?"

"A hundred and twenty-three dollars and fifty-one cents."

Jamie regarded him shrewdly. Tom could tell he was impressed.

"Well, what do you think?" Tom asked.

"I'm thinking that's enough to buy my corner," Jamie said.

"Really?"

"Well, I'll think about it while you get the money. That is, if you really have the money."

"Wait a minute," Tom said. "That money includes the squeegees and the bucket, right?"

Jamie smiled and gestured eloquently toward the bucket.

Tom ran to the bus depot to get the money from his locker. He was sure Jamie would be gone when he got back, but he wasn't. It was almost dark by the time the transaction was complete. Tom picked up his inventory, as Jamie had called it, and paid Jeans a visit.

"I found a job," Tom said. "Self-employment."

"Say again?"

"Windows. I used my money to get us these." Tom tossed over the two squeegees. "You're welcome to come in on it with me." Jeans stared at them and didn't bend to touch one.

"Squeegees," Tom said.

"I know that."

"You stand on a busy street corner and—"

"I know. I know that."

"Oh," said Tom.

"I been here a long while. I tried it once." Jeans pointed at nothing. "If you lucky, people point. If you lucky, people pay, don't give you six cents. On a bad day, you jump 'em, but most times then they don't pay. They jus' scowl at you for cleanin' up their pretty car. You make twenty, maybe thirty dollars a good day, nothing or ten on a bad day. One day you get lucky, you make a hundred dollars. Keeps you goin', but it took all my squeegee money jus' to stay street lovin'."

"Paid ten dollars a day to stay in a junk place with six others. I figured that landlord gettin' twenty-one hundred dollars a month for a two-bedroom shack with big ol' beetles in the cupboards and a stove that shock you every time you stir the pot. The ten dollars left got me burgers and ice cream. Job like this," Jeans pushed one of the squeegees with the toe of his foot, "just keep you street lovin'."

Jeans sat down into the down-coat nest. Feathers flew.

Tom sat down. No feathers.

"Hope they didn't cost you much," Jeans said.

"Oh. No."

"You go ahead," Jeans said. "Maybe they like the look of you better."

Tom shook his head. They both sat in silence a long time, staring at the squeegees.

"I miss home," Jeans said.

Tom sighed. "Me, too."

"You think we ever get home?" Jeans asked.

Tom thought Jeans looked about nine years old at that moment. "We'll get home," Tom said.

"Yeah? How do you know that?" His voice cracked.

Tom got out his book. He opened it and started writing.

"What?" Jeans said. "What are you writin'?"

"Says: **Jeans bought a plane ticket and went back to Jamaica.**"

"Oh, man," Jeans said. "You got a talent there. A talent, is what I say." He sighed and sank down into the coats. He didn't talk much after that.

Tom left. When he tried to sell the squeegees back to Betty Jamie Boop, the kid laughed and shook his head. "Sorry, Lipstick Licker. I already invested the capital. I'm in big business now. Speaking of which, you want some Forget?" Tom left the bucket and walked away without answering. He was back to needing $5,388.

The next day Tom looked for HELP WANTED signs in windows again.

Over the next few weeks, he got odd jobs, deliveries, inventory, but nothing permanent. And nothing Jeans could do. Jeans couldn't work indoors. Evenings Tom hung out at the LRT stations, shelters, parks, bars, looking for Daniel. Most days Samuel Wolflegs would be sitting on the bench in the park with a sandwich or fruit or a chocolate bar. Samuel thought Daniel had quit smoking and Tom should find different bait.

Tom tried saving his chocolate bars for bait, which also did not work. But every day Samuel would remind Tom that he was a Finder. "You have evil magic enough in your lives, you kids," Samuel would say. "You need good magic to fight it."

Some mornings Tom thought maybe it wasn't true, but every night, whether he found something or not, he knew it had to be true even if it wasn't. Some mornings, what was true was that he smelled and his clothes looked like he had slept on the ground all night.

He showered at the Greyhound station when Tuba was on duty. Once in a while, he exchanged clothes at the Sally Ann. He occasionally got food at the soup kitchen, but he didn't like that people looked at him there. He could always count on Samuel having something for him.

"Hey, aren't you having any today?" Tom asked Samuel one afternoon while he ate a cheese sandwich.

Samuel shook his head.

It occurred to Tom that he had never seen Samuel eat. At the same time it registered that the man had lost weight. "You on a diet or something?"

Samuel looked at the river. "My son is not eating tonight."

"What?"

Samuel looked at him.

"You mean you're not eating until I find Daniel?" He stared at Samuel, then at his sandwich, and threw the rest of it into the river. The baby geese, almost grown now, devoured it. "You're zoid, you know that. You know that? You're going to quit eating until I find your kid . . . ?"

"You are a Finder."

"What if I'm not?" Tom shouted. The geese on the river half-swam, half-flew away. "If I was a Finder, wouldn't I have found Daniel by now, and my parents, and a freaking million bucks?"

Samuel had on that blissful believer's face that Tom had seen before. Tom swore and ran away as fast as he could.

That night he didn't sleep on the island. He slept under the bridge and was so tired he hardly woke up when the old man came through yelling, "Ghosts, ghosts!"

In the morning he looked for Janice. He wanted to run some of his writing by her, see what she thought, see if she laughed at the part where it said Tom was a Finder. He found her and Pam, standing in front of a window. Pam was braless under a T-shirt that said THE TRUE NORTH STRONG AND FREE. Janice was scratching her thigh. "Shelter rash," she said as Tom approached. Seeing Pam made him forget why he'd come looking for Janice.

The mannequins were all wearing black. Each one was carrying a wineglass. Tom stood beside Pam and looked in the window with her for what seemed a long time before she noticed him. Finally, she turned her attention to him and smiled. Tom wondered how you went about becoming prime minister.

She gestured to the window. "This would be good if they were selling wineglasses. Your eye focuses on them." She walked along the window. "There's really people like that, you know, people who dress so fine and wear diamonds. We just don't see them much. But these windows—it's like a peepshow into their world."

"How can they have fun, knowing there's us?" Janice asked.

Pam looked at her thoughtfully. Tom silently promised himself he'd ask his parents about that when he got home.

"I do that a lot," Janice said. "Throw cold water on a potentially good time. It's a gift." She took a step closer to Tom. "You're still not one of us," she said.

"Janice," Pam murmured.

"He's not. You can see it in his eyes." She stepped away and said, "I'm going to check out the baby clothes."

When she was gone, Pam grinned at him. "You busy?"

"Busy looking at you."

She rolled her eyes, then smiled again. "I'll take you on a tour."

He took her hand. "Okay, let's go," he said. Tom was amazed at himself. Was he good at girls before? He must have been. Things were coming back.

Pam led him on a tour of all the display windows she loved best: men's clothing, women's clothing, children's clothing, hats, shoes, bags and briefcases, umbrellas, scarves and gloves, hardware, houseware, plants, pets, wedding, bedding, watches . . .

They went into some stores, played on computers, listened to CDs, played with the toys, read all the greeting cards.

"Some stores are for smelling," Pam said. They stood in front of bakeries, coffee shops, soup spoons, pretzel and popcorn booths, hotdog stands, cigar shops, soap and perfume places. They stood outside the Crispy Chicken place, and Pam told him that smelling was ninety percent of tasting.

"Does this make you happy?" he asked Pam. "Window-shopping?"

She nodded. "But it baffles me," she continued. "All there is in the world. Like there's this world of shopping, but it's not a world for me. It's for looking, smelling, wishing, sometimes touching—but not for having or buying. Do you know what I mean?"

"Kind of," he said. "Sometimes I think the world of the street is the only real world. All the rest is a story, with characters moving around on the pages, but not really having anything to do with me."

She stared at him.

"Yeah," he continued. "Except sometimes the characters—they speak in whispers to me, like dialogue on a page, but I can't talk back, no more than I could jump into the pages of a book. It's there, I can see it, but I can't figure out how to be a part of it."

Pam faced him. "See," she said. "That's why you're a poet, Tom, because you can say things people are feeling that they can't say for themselves."

She hugged him. For two long seconds she pressed up against him, and her hair smelled like the soap store.

"Pam," he said. "About this new boyfriend. Janice says he's a . . . not a nice person."

"Um . . . in case you didn't notice, Janice is one bootie short of a pair."

He said, "I have some money, if you need it."

"Gotta go, Mr. Poet," she said. He watched her vanish into the crowds until someone bumped him hard. It was a young man, big, but clean-cut and well-dressed. He shook his finger at Tom, and walked after Pam.

Cupid, Tom thought. He'd been watching her.

The starlight on the river was so bright that he could see to write in his book. Pam had inspired him. He wrote: **Tom found a job. Two jobs. Everything's going to be okay.** Then his moat sang him to sleep.

The next morning Tom found the jobs hanging by cables outside the Agcor Building. Two men suspended in a cage were washing windows. Tom watched for three hours until the men finally touched down.

Tom approached them, standing with his best posture.

"Excuse me, but I'm looking for—"

"A kick in the pants if you don't get lost," one of the men said without looking at him. Tom wished he would look at him so he could see how straight he was standing, how perfect his posture was. The man had dreadlocks halfway down his back, braided with beads. The other man was shiny bald. His ear had been tattooed into a screaming mouth. The ear hole was the throat of the mouth.

"I'm looking for a job. Two jobs. One for me, one for my friend."

"You got a friend?" asked Dreadlocks, and Tattoo laughed. "How old are you?"

Tom guessed, "Um . . . eighteen? My friend's probably . . . um . . . twenty-one. We've got window experience."

"Oh. Okay. Sure. Whatever you say."

"What's your name, kid?" Dreadlocks asked.

"Tom."

"Tom what?"

Tom shrugged.

"Maybe you should be looking for a real name," Tattoo said.

Tom stood still as if waiting for a more intelligent answer.

"Gotta have guts to do this job," Dreadlocks said.

"I've got guts," Tom said. He couldn't remember if he had guts, but he could fight and swim and he had a way with girls. He didn't think they'd care if he could spell.

Tattoo was getting irritated. "Kid, where's your mommy? Go home."

"I am home. This is where I live."

"In the Agcor Building?"

"No. Here. On the streets."

"In the Core?"

Tom nodded.

Tattoo shook his head. "Guess you do have guts, then. Just no brains."

"Listen. I'm a writer. I'll write an article about you, about skyscraper window cleaners. It'll be great for business. You let me and my friend come for a day to research. If you don't like us, then don't give us a job."

Dreadlocks laughed. "Come back tomorrow and we'll talk."

That night Tom returned to the park and Jeans's tree. He climbed and found Jeans lying on the coats, staring up into the leaves with his hands behind his head.

"I'm dreamin' of chicken soup," he said without looking at Tom.

Tom got himself all the way onto the platform. He liked it up here, but wondered how Jeans didn't roll off the platform in the night while he slept. He lay back in the coats. "Jeans, I am a poet."

"You say what?"

Tom sat up. "A poet. What I write changes things."

"Oh," Jeans said. Then, after a moment, "You know how to make chicken soup?"

"Yes. You go to the store and buy a can of—"

"No, I mean real chicken soup. You know how, Tom?"

"No."

"I do."

"How then?" Tom asked, laying back into the coats.

"First you get a chicken. Then you chop off his head and break off his feet and pull out his guts and pluck out the feathers, and then you boil it. My mama used to make the best chicken soup. You like chicken soup, Tom?"

"Used to." Tom was pretty sure his mom made homemade chicken soup. It wasn't a memory, just an assumption based on what he knew she'd be like. *Assumption.* You had to have great parents to know a word like that.

They were silent for a time, listening to the wind in the leaves. Wolflegs was right about sitting on grass and under trees. It made his stomach relax.

Finally, he couldn't keep the news to himself anymore. "I found us a job out of doors," he said.

Jeans sat up.

Tom yawned before he continued. "Washing windows on the skyscrapers."

"For real?"

"Well, they're going to give us a trial day. They said come tomorrow. You've gotta have guts to do the job."

Jeans laughed. "Man, you a poet. Everythin' you say is jus' poetry to my ears. How come you not smilin'? How come you never smile? Man, you making my backside smile. Come on. Show me the place. I wanna see it tonight."

They climbed down the tree and splashed in the waterfall.

Tom wished he could smile. He wanted to. Bad. He was so happy that he wasn't even tempted to steal the coins. After, they ran the streets until they were dry.

They were almost at the Agcor when they saw a group of seven boys coming toward them, walking together like they owned the street.

"The Perfs," Jeans said. "My gang."

One of them was big, way over six feet tall and wide in the shoulders and chest.

"Hey, Jeans!" he called.

"That's Sasky," Jeans said. "Jus' be polite and do what he say and everything be okay."

"Sasky?" Tom whispered.

"Don't know if he is called that because he from Saskatchewan, or 'cause he the Sasquatch."

The boys stopped and stood around them in a circle.

"Where you Been, Jeans? You got a new Gang?" His mouth was grinning amiably, but his body was frowning. His muscles were fisted up. Tom decided he'd be polite.

"No, man. I been hangin' with Tom. He is a poet." Tom modestly dropped his head and shoved his hands in his pockets.

"A Poet." Sasky said, as if trying to remember what that was.

Tom thought he could smell male hormones in the air, and they weren't his.

"Yeah. That mean he got a hole in his head," Jeans said, laughing. "He qualify to be a Perf."

Tom shifted his weight from one foot to the other. Gravitational attraction depended on mass. Sasky only weighed more because of stupid gravity. Tom could see the pavement was still soft and tarry from the hot day. He played with the change in his pocket.

"Do I hear Jingles in your pockets?" Sasky asked. He held out a huge hand. "Guess you better hand 'em over before you go."

It was a friendly gesture: just hand me your change as a small token of submission and we'll be okay with you. Tom didn't mind submission. It was the money he couldn't part with.

Sasky stood still with his hand out. Tom couldn't hear anyone breathing.

"Can't," he said without looking up from the pavement.

Sasky's hand made a fist.

"Can't?" someone said. Tom realized it was Jeans speaking, but in a choked kind of voice.

There was a restless movement among the boys, as if up to that moment they'd been sleeping on their feet.

"Can't," said Tom. "I'm saving."

"Saving?" Sasky growled.

"For my billboard."

There was a deep silence for a moment before Sasky laughed. Then they all laughed.

"You're right, Jeans. This boy has got a Hole in his head."

Jeans laughed. Sasky laughed. The boys laughed.

The laughter stopped. "Okay, kid. Hand over the Toonies and

get Outta Here." There was real danger in his voice, more capitalized letters.

Tom shrugged. *Tom can fight.*

"I'm gonna have to Beat you up for a Few Toonies?" Sasky asked with real disgust in his voice.

Tom looked up, looked Sasky right in his eyes. He found that he could—if he held his nose up just like that—he could smell his own hormones too. Poet hormones. "You'll have to catch me first," he said.

In that moment Tom's face remembered how to smile.

Sasky and Tom stood grinning at one another with eyes like animals.

And then they were running: Tom silent, smooth-moving, brains in his feet; Sasky hooting, leaping, swearing, laughing.

"Hoo, man, hear those Toonies calling to Me!" he shouted after Tom.

Tom, smelling the way, laughed a great, loud, breathless laugh. The soft, tarry streets bounced his feet, but made it sticky for Sasky, slowing him down. The streets love me, Tom thought.

"Gonna buy me some Export A's with your Toonies," Sasky called. "Gonna stuff your Underwear in your Mouth. Gonna get me some Doughnuts and gum and sit on your head while I chew. Gonna make you an official member . . ."

Tom laughed again. He knew he was getting away when he couldn't hear the capitals on Sasky's words anymore.

Tom ran all the way to his island. Samuel wasn't there. He walked along the river until his heart slowed, then wrapped himself in his blanket.

Tom has guts, he wrote in his book, and then laughed himself to sleep.

The next morning Tom was wakened by rain on his face. The sun was shining too. It was like the cloud was only over his head. He washed at Fas Gas, and found buns and oatmeal cookies in the bakery dumpster. He took some of the cookies to Jeans, who was already waiting for him at the bench in the park.

Tom saw that he had a fat lip. Jeans pointed to his mouth. "This is Sasky bein' irate with me because of you."

"Sorry," Tom said. "But look, I can smile."

"Why, 'cause you cheated death? Nobody talk to Sasky like that, even if he a poet. You run if you see him again. He catch you, he perforate you for real." Then Jeans smiled. "However, I do thank you for the memory."

As they walked to the job, Jeans told Tom he'd sworn off his gang anyway.

"They say, oh, you so safe with us, we gonna protect you from the bad guys, we gonna give you respect, we gonna be your family. 'Cept I find out they just salesmen, you know. Never had enemies till I got a gang. Never got respect from them, only bein' scared. Like las' night. Had enough. If they my family, I am leavin' home."

"You don't have to do that for me," Tom said.

"Don't you go thinkin' like that. Don't like you that much."

The window washers had already completed their first drop for the day by the time Tom and Jeans arrived. They waved them over.

"I wasn't sure you'd be working in the rain," Tom said.

Dreadlocks's hair hung like dripping rags down his back. "We work in the rain, in the dark, in the cold. The only time we don't work is when it's windy. Wind shears come down between the buildings like they do in a canyon. So, you think you're up for this?"

"We up," Jeans said.

"We'll give you a taste. Come on."

In the stage were squeegees, buckets, horsehair brushes, a cell phone, and a ghetto blaster, all attached to the stage by strings.

"Idiot strings," Dreadlocks said. "Falling from this height, even a brush could kill somebody."

"Gravity does that," Tom said.

"I'm flyin'!" Jeans said, lifting his arms.

Tom eyed the four pencil-thin cables that held the stage, then looked over the edge. The speed of gravity's pull does not depend on what you weigh, Tom remembered. If there were no air, a feather would fall as fast as a brick. He gripped the stage. It was far enough down that you'd have time to curse yourself before you hit the ground. Tom held his head up so he could smell his own hormones.

"It takes six hours to complete a single drop," Dreadlocks said as he worked the windows. "We get paid by the window, so the quicker you work, the better. Try it."

He handed the squeegee to Tom, who took twice as long to do one window and did only half as good a job, even though he was trying twice as hard.

"You'll get the hang of it," Dreadlocks said. "As you go, inspect the skin of the building. Note any stone chips, air leaks, lost caulking. Your turn, kid."

He handed the squeegee to Jeans, but Jeans was staring at Tom's chest as if he had just seen a big, ugly spider. Tom looked down. There *was* a spider—a loonie-sized spider, and that didn't include the legs. Tom didn't have the nerve to brush it off.

"Hey, that Spiderman's little brother?" Jeans asked nervously.

Then one landed on Jeans. Jeans was turning green under his brown skin, which made him look khaki-colored.

"That's what these air vacs are for," Dreadlocks said. He took the handheld vacuum cleaner and sucked up the spiders, then grabbed one that landed on the stage floor. "They spin their webs on the high walls and feed off flies in the air currents," he said. "Okay, kid, your turn. Can't let the creepy-crawlies slow you down."

Jeans was better at it than Tom. They took half-hour turns. By the time they touched ground, Tom's shoulder and arm were sore. It hurt just to dangle his arm.

"'It's a good hurt," Jeans said. "Idle jackass follows a cane stalk into the pound, my mama always say."

"Didn't scare you off, boys?" Dreadlocks asked.

Jeans said no.

Dreadlocks laughed. "Come back tomorrow and I might pay you."

The next day Jeans paired off with Tattoo and Tom with Dreadlocks. They got paid fifty cents a window, and Tom counted all the way down. He and Jeans did two drops that day. At the end of the day, Tom's arm and shoulders and back and neck were in so much pain that it made him nauseous. Jeans got tears in his eyes when he tried to wave at Tom, but he kept smiling. Dreadlocks said they did okay and come back tomorrow.

Before he went back to his island, Tom looked for Daniel. That night Wolflegs was there on his bench. He wasn't doing well against gravity. His eyes drooped at the corners, and his jaw was slack. His coat sagged on him.

"Anderson Station today," Tom said, sitting on the bench. "Samuel, I'm sorry about the other day. You know, about you not eating. You can eat now. I think I really am a Finder. I found a real job, and one for my friend. It's amazing. But it had something to do with writing things down in this book. I'm not sure how it works, or why—"

"Tom, go home," Wolflegs said.

Tom could smell the alcohol from the other side of the bench.

"I haven't found home yet," Tom said.

"You aren't looking hard enough. You should be looking for home, not for my boy."

"Well, I am saving up for a billboard. Besides, you said I wouldn't find home until I found Daniel—"

"Think you're so tough, just like my Daniel. Nothing on the streets can hurt me, you think. You're mostly right. It's not what's on the street that destroys you. It's what you're running from. Running away instead of fighting. Or fighting everything and everyone except what you should be fighting. What are you running from, Tom? Mother? Father? No mother? No father? School? Chicken skins, every one of you." Wolflegs pushed Tom off the bench. "Not one warrior among you. Go home, fight for yourself, make yourself face your battles. Scared. Running scared and thinking you're so tough."

Wolflegs threw up. All liquid. No chunks. He still wasn't eating. Tom didn't know a human stomach could hold that much fluid. He thought for sure he was going to be sick himself just from the stench.

Wolflegs stumbled into his own puke and lay there moaning, praying, praying to the river.

Tom didn't remember what you were supposed to do with drunks, but he remembered he was nice. He wasn't sure, right then, what nice was. It wasn't bad, but maybe it wasn't great. Would nice help the guy up?

Tom helped Wolflegs up. He helped him to the river to clean him up, then helped him back to the bench. Wolflegs was silent the whole time. Tom sat him on the bench, braids dripping. The book was true. He was nice. This was total proof.

"It's okay," Tom said gently. "You can start eating. I am going to find him." He walked away. Before he was out of earshot, Tom heard Samuel start to snore.

That night he wrote an article on high-rise window washing for the newspaper man, and fell asleep dreaming about how the world would reward him.

Chapter 7

Once again, do not forget the word "silence."
— Act 2, scene 13

The next morning Jeans met him, thin and shoe-polish black. He was singing a Jamaican song.

"You're happy," Tom said.

"I am thinkin' about how pretty I will look for Gina."

Later, while working, Tom looked for Daniel from the stage until Dreadlocks swore at him.

That evening Jeans went with him when he deposited the money Dreadlocks had given him in the Greyhound locker. They showered in the station washrooms and went in search of food in the dumpsters.

"Dreadlocks talkin' like they going to get the owner to put us on paychecks like regular taxpayers," Jeans said to Tom. "All you gotta do is fill out a few forms, SIN number and stuff, and go to the cops for a piece of paper sayin' you got no record, he says."

Jeans and Tom looked at each other. "I like it the way it's been," Tom said.

"Me too," Jeans said. "Come on. I'm gonna introduce you to some of my friends," Jeans said. "Nice people, the kindliest on the street. Girl fish. Come on."

"Girl fish?"

"Yeah. They on the hook, dyin' for air."

Jeans led him to the part of town where the girls hung out. Tom had seen a few of them before. He thought they were beautiful in a sad kind of way, like a fancy streetlight with a few bulbs burnt out.

"Jeans, I don't think—"

"Yes. That is so."

"There's nobody here I want to get to know."

Jeans stopped and put his hand on Tom's shoulder. "You go, then. But before you do, Mr. Poet, there's a thing or two you got to learn yet. That liddle girl," he said, pointing to one who was anything but little, "she jus' like any other liddle girl, 'cept she got on the streets. Does not matter how. Some, it is more dangerous at home. Some, they jus' don't see how all the pieces of their life fit together, like a big puzzle spilled out on the table. So they try Forget to help them figure it out. They don't know every time they do that, a piece gets lost. Pretty soon, they don't think they much to give away. Now don't you go worryin'. We just talkin', okay? And lookin'. That's all I do. That's why they my friends, see."

Jeans approached three women standing on the corner. He introduced them to Tom as Martha and Gladys and Beatrice. Jeans and the women started joking and laughing. Tom held back a little, his hands in his pockets.

"Tell your fortune," a young voice said from a recessed door-way.

Tom looked around and saw a girl. Pam.

"What . . . what are you doing here?"

"Starting my own business," she said. "Telling fortunes that are sheer poetry." She smiled. Tom thought maybe he was supposed to say: Great Wonderful That's Just Great.

He couldn't speak. She was dressed in red spandex shorts and a white halter top with a maple leaf on it. Just looking at her made Tom want to sing "O Canada." It also made him want to throw a blanket over her head and carry her away to his parents' house. He made himself smile politely.

"I never saw you smile before," she said.

"I just learned," Tom said. "No job, I guess."

"I had one at the doughnut place, but they fired me for letting Janice sleep at the table."

"You still trying to go to school?"

She shrugged again. "Someone stole my alarm clock. I've been late a bunch of times, and they put me on probation." She looked down at her fortune-teller and moved her fingers. It looked like it was talking to her, but no sound was coming out. "My boyfriend ripped up my English textbook."

Tom shoved his fists into his pockets.

"He felt bad," she said. "Drove me to school the next day. It's just that . . . you know . . . he dreams so big, but there's just not enough for all of his dreams."

"Why don't you go back to the shelter?" He let just a little of his anger out, just for a moment, but then he couldn't stop it. "Why, Pam? Why don't you Do Something?" He was talking in capitals like Sasky.

She nodded. "The shelter."

Tom shrugged. "It's better than nothing. Go home, then."

"You don't know my mother." Pam's voice had an edge to it. "I'm not doing anything wrong. I tell fortunes for five bucks." She snapped the fortune-teller, the piece of paper folded into little hoods that moved when she moved her fingers. "Want to?"

"I don't have any money on me," Tom said.

She rolled her eyes. "The cute ones never do. Come here then. I'll do it for free."

Tom came closer. She smelled faintly of maple sugar. "How come you like Janice?"

"Because she's kind." Pam looked at him. "What, you think it's strange to like her because she's zoidy? Well, I think if any of us had any sense, we'd all be like that."

This was a hard concept for Tom, who had just learned how to smile.

"Anyway, I haven't seen her in a while. She said some bad things about my boyfriend. But he's changed. He's going to change. For me. She doesn't believe me. Besides, I don't have to stay at the shelter anymore. When Cupid's crazy, I've got friends with places. Sometimes I stay at the old Spaghetti Factory. You should come. We light fires in there. People are nice. We look out for each other."

"No thanks," Tom said. "Too many people. Too much roof."

She studied him. "Maybe Janice is right about you, that you're not one of us. I don't know how . . . Maybe it's because of you being a poet and stuff."

"I never said that."

"You act it. But I say you are one of us, because none of us think it either. We all think we're going to quit it someday and be a plumber or a hairdresser, don't you know that?"

"Do you think it, Pam?"

Pam's eyes stayed on him, but she wasn't seeing him anymore. "I don't know. I don't know myself anymore. It's like I looked myself into one of those windows and I can't get out, and everyone's staring at me and I can't figure out why they don't help me."

"I'll help," Tom said.

She was seeing him again. She smiled. "Hey. It's okay. I'm tough. Besides, I'm in school, remember? Pick a color."

"Pink. That's good—about school, I mean."

"P–I–N–K. Pick another color. I only need three courses to graduate."

"Red. You can do it. I'll help you with English. And science maybe."

"R–E–D. Thanks. Pick a number."

"Three."

She took the hoods off her fingers and unfolded one corner. Tom could see that the paper was blank. She slowly ran her finger along the edge of the paper. A small drop of blood appeared. She smeared it on the paper, then stared at the paper a long time without saying a word.

She's zoid, too, Tom thought.

"Paper cut," she said. "I don't do that for everybody."

Tom knew it—he did have a way with girls. You either had it or you didn't. It wasn't something you could fake.

"Strange," she said.

Tom peered over her fortune-teller, but he couldn't see anything but bloodstained paper. "What?"

"Without a past, the future is not written except by today," she said in a spooky voice.

"Huh?"

"Wait," she said. "Something to do with music—an opera maybe."

"An opera?"

Just then they heard Jeans calling loudly, "Hey, Cupid! How's it layin', man?"

From down the street, Cupid answered in a deep voice, "To the left." He said something else that they couldn't hear.

Pam stood straight. "Go," she said.

Tom could see Jeans doing some sort of dance in front of Cupid, and they were both laughing.

"Go!" Pam said, sinking back into the shadows.

Tom walked away. Jeans caught up with him after a while, panting.

"Thanks," Tom said.

"Were for Pam."

"You told her about me, didn't you," Tom said when they had gone a block or two.

"Not much. You borin'."

"You told her about the opera, didn't you."

"No."

"Did."

"Didn't."

"Then how'd she know?"

Jeans kicked a can on the sidewalk. "Pam. Everyone knows, she got the gift."

"Why does she hang out on the streets, with those other girls?"

"They her friends."

"No way."

Jeans stopped and faced Tom. "They also my friends."

Tom shifted his backpack a little. "Did I say anything?"

"I hear the disrespect in your voice."

Tom didn't deny it.

"I seen a thing you have not seen, Tom Poet. When you sold your last possession, when you eatin' other people's garbage, when you cold and dirty and so tired you sleep in public, then tell me you won't have nothin' to do with a guy who smile and say you wonderful and gonna love you forever. Then one day, he down on his luck, and if you really love him, you gonna do him a favor. The girls, they all think their boyfriend gonna get back on his feet, gonna take them to Disneyland with that john money. Then the boyfriend, he beat them. She understand. He jealous, all those men gettin' a piece of her. But he need the money. Just a little longer, that's all."

"Then one day, she know. She know, and nothin' matter much, least of all herself. She don't save. She don't wanna look at that john money any longer than she have to. She spend it on food and a place to sleep, and a Forget so's she can face the life again. She learn to survive, and she learn not to care too bad if she don't."

Tom walked in silence beside Jeans. His feet hit the pavement as if he weighed three hundred pounds. "Does Pam . . . is she thinking . . . ?"

"Not turned out yet. But all her friends, they on the street. She couch-surfin' right now."

They had arrived at the park.

"See you in the morning," Tom said. Jeans didn't look back and wave like he usually did.

As he walked to his island, Tom wondered if there was any up or down in the universe. Was it only gravity that invented up and down? All he knew was that gravity ruled the world, kept everything down. You had to fight to get anywhere.

Tom stared at the billboard on the way home. THE MAGIC FLUTE, SEPTEMBER 12–15. Tom checked the electronic sign. SEPTEMBER 8. He'd been here a long time. Maybe he just wasn't a good enough writer.

Chapter 8

I know how to deal with nets and snares.
And how to make myself understood by piping.
— Act 1, scene 2

"So it's you. You look pretty rough." The newspaper man had loosened his tie and taken off his jacket. He bent his face back to the sun.

"I do?"

"Just getting the last bits of summer." He glanced at Tom. "Gets pretty cool in the fall, you know. Where do you go when it's cold?"

"Oh, I'll have things worked out by then," Tom said.

The man said nothing for a minute, then gestured. "So, what have you got there?"

Tom looked down at the paper in his hand. He held it out to the man. "I thought you might read this, tell me if it's any good."

The man sat up and roughly snatched the papers, bending and wrinkling them. "Let's see."

He read for a while. "Use a dictionary?" he asked.

"No."

"Should use a dictionary. For spelling."

"Did I misspell something?"

"No."

"I didn't think so. Well?"

"Interesting." He hit the paper with his knuckles. "Always wondered about those guys. I like the part about the spiders. I'll buy it."

"For . . . for money?"

The man tightened his tie and put his jacket on. "Next time do it up on a computer, will ya? I'll have a check made up for you."

"I'd like cash, please," Tom said.

The man groomed his mustache a moment, then reached for his wallet. "I'm buying a career here," he said gruffly.

Career, Tom thought. *I have a career.* C–A–R–E–E–R.

Tom was walking away when the man called, "What's your byline?"

"Tom," Tom called back. "Tom Finder."

"Where you go at night?" Jeans asked Tom the next day.

"I'm looking for someone."

"Daniel still?"

"Yeah. I'm going to a men's shelter tonight, check it out."

"Them gray, roofy places, Tom."

"It's okay. I can write, remember? Come with me."

Jeans nodded.

The Drop-in Shelter for Homeless Men was full of men who rarely looked up. Gravity had got to them.

It had gotten into their ear holes and filled their brains. It made their heads hang down and their hair hang down and their hands hang down and made their eyes always look at their feet. It made them slow-moving. Their words fell out of their mouths. You didn't get to a drop-in center by floating or flying or climbing, or even by walking. You dropped in, gravity's baby.

Tom figured if you stayed on the streets long enough, eventually you just couldn't fight it anymore. It probably felt good after a while not to fight anymore. You just let it press you down.

Jeans said, "Pretty close walls in this place."

Tom nodded.

"Yup," Jeans said. "Pretty close."

Tom knew how you could be all right to be here. Sometimes, at night, alone in the dark, Tom felt gravity sitting on his chest, like an animal perched there. At first it felt okay because you had air in there, but after a while you had less air and soon you couldn't breathe. Maybe one day that was all you could do anymore: sleep pinned to your cot, and it didn't matter where.

One of the volunteers was speaking to a man who looked like he'd been sat on by gravity one too many times.

"You know the stains on the pavement better than you know your own face, Jenks," the volunteer said.

Jenks didn't smile. He mumbled something incomprehensible. Tom remembered him. He was the old man under the bridge, the man who saw ghosts everywhere.

"Takes more muscles to frown than to smile," the volunteer said. Maybe it took fewer muscles to smile, Tom thought, but those smiling muscles had to work against gravity. Besides, Jenks wasn't really frowning. Tom could tell he was just letting gravity pull his face down.

"Can I help you?" the volunteer said to Tom and Jeans.

"I'm looking for Daniel Wolflegs," Tom said.

"Haven't seen him for a long time," the man said. "Need a bed tonight?"

Tom shook his head. Jeans shook his head.

"I seen him," Jenks said.

"Where?" Tom asked.

"With the dead," Jenks said. "Floating."

Jeans made a sign with his left hand.

"Never mind him," Tom said. "He sees ghosts everywhere."

"You'll never find him if you don't look among the dead," he said.

"Yeah? Where do I go for that?" Tom asked.

"You don't wanna go there, where the dead are. Don't wanna go there."

Tom felt all the little hairs on his back lift up like antennae.

"Where?" Tom asked again.

"You won't find him," Jenks said.

"I have to," Tom said. He had to for the book to be true. He had to if he was going to find his parents.

"He's been sick," Jenks said. "Acorn took care of him."

"Acorn? Where do I find him?" Tom asked.

"Her. No address. Over the bridge, but doesn't have an address."

Then he shuffled away.

"Come on," Tom said. He left with Jeans close behind him.

When they were out, Jeans leaned against the wall. Sweat was dripping from his hair.

"I'm going to find this Acorn person," Tom said. "Coming?"

Jeans shook his head. "I meet you later," he said weakly. "Gonna see my girl fish." He walked away.

Tom crossed the bridge and walked among the houses south of the river. He didn't have any idea where he was going. But he was the Finder. He had the power. He concentrated on Daniel, on everything he knew about Daniel, on the things Samuel had told him about his son. He knew of a row of small, rotting houses just past the bridge. He'd start there.

He walked past house after house, knowing each house wasn't it. At the end of a long block that ended near the river, he stopped. There was something strange—the last house had a huge yard, and the walkway seemed to be too far to the right of the house. He couldn't see in for all the trees. Tom stood for a time, then turned into the walkway. Instead of curving in toward the house, it curved in the other direction.

The walkway was overhung by branches. The roots of the trees broke up the cement blocks of the walkway. Soon the walkway was almost completely covered in pine cones and old pine needles. The trees were so large that he couldn't see the house until he was right on it. It was a log house, and the door was ajar. Bats flew around a large kerosene lamp that sat on the porch.

Tom called into the door, "Hello! Anyone here?" He could hear a woman humming. "Hello?"

A girl with green hair emerged from the shadows, carrying a candle. "Welcome," she said.

"I'm sorry. It must be late."

"Peace," she said. "Something brings you here. Come, sit down."

She led him into a room full of ferns and tropical plants. There was a bamboo curtain, and cushions everywhere. A yellow and green bird chirped on a kind of swing. There was no cage.

"Are you Acorn?" Tom asked.

"I am," she said. "How did you find me?"

"I am a Finder," Tom said. He figured anyone with a name like Acorn could handle it. A fountain burbled in the corner, and Tom could see there was a turtle in it. Two cats jumped up and ran away as Tom sat down. "I'm looking for Daniel Wolflegs," he said. "I heard he comes here sometimes."

She sat cross-legged on a cushion and put the candle in front of her. She stared at the flame. "Yes. He comes here. He's not here now. What do you need him for?"

How could he explain what he needed Daniel for? Because finding him would make true what he thought about himself. Because finding Daniel meant he could do anything in the world, and gravity didn't win. Because finding Daniel meant he was a poet.

"His dad asked me to find him," he said simply, and that was true, too. "He's been looking for him for a long time."

She shifted on her cushion. "Daniel is my friend. I'm pretty sure he doesn't want to see his dad."

"His dad loves him. He'll die looking for him. Samuel is . . . good."

"He passed on his genes, then," Acorn said, smiling. "There's no one like Daniel. Drugs sometimes make people mean. They just make Daniel softer. I think he's dying. I think he's dying because some people want him to. He's obliging that way." She tilted her head. "Why do you care? What do you get out of it?"

Tom could see that he had to answer this question, and the answer had better be right. He took out his notebook, opened it, and began to read. The pages were a bit damp. Twice he looked up. Once Acorn was softly nodding her head, as if agreeing. The second time her eyes were closed and she was very still. While he read, both cats and a big dog came into the room and settled on cushions around him. It was quiet except for the whine of mosquitoes and the breeze in the trees outside.

He closed the book.

After a moment, she said, "There's an old man named Jenks. Daniel was kind to him, protected him from some drunk teenagers who thought it would be fun to torment him. Jenks takes care of Daniel, when he's sober. He'd probably know where he is."

"Jenks? But he's the one who told me to come here."

She shook her head. "Just trying to get rid of you maybe. He'll know where to find Daniel."

Tom found Pam, fortune-teller in hand, on the baby stroll. He'd run the whole way.

"You don't have the cops after you, do you?" She was wearing tight shortie shorts and a belly shirt that said SAVE THE BEAVERS. "I don't have a business license." She laughed.

Jeans saw him and came over. "Find Daniel?"

"No. The girl said Jenks knows, but that old drunk doesn't know anything."

"Hey," Pam said, smiling. "Be nice."

Tom didn't feel like smiling right now. Right now, he was angry to find her here again, talking to the other women like they were friends, like she was one of them.

"In business? What about school?"

"I quit," she said, hard, as if she was swearing. She looked at him as if she were a foot taller than him.

"Why don't you go home?" Tom asked. But he wasn't asking, he was ordering. "Why don't you ditch stupid Cupid and go home. You remember: H–O–M–E."

Pam stared at him. Jeans stared at him. Jeans broke out in loud, uncomfortable laughter. He punched Tom in the arm, hard. "You know these poet-types, heh, heh. You never know what outbursts they gonna have. Not their fault," he said confidingly to Pam and pointing meaningfully to his head. " 'Sides, he goin' nuts lookin' for his friend Daniel Wolflegs. You seen him, Pam? No? Well, gotta go—"

"Check the abandoned Spaghetti Factory," she said. "Squats a lot of kids these days. Landfill. Janice is there now, too." She clicked her paper fortune-teller over Tom's head. "Hey, mister, tell your fortune."

"Just tell me I'm gonna get lucky," a man said behind Tom.

Tom didn't look back. He and Jeans just moved out of the way.

"Man, you got a way with words," Jeans said to him after they had walked awhile. "But not always a good way."

Tom felt sick. What had happened to nice? To being good with girls? And where were his parents? Why hadn't they flooded the media with pictures, pleas for public assistance? "Tom is a good boy, he'd never run away. Please help us find our son." He had to think of something true right now, or he was going to think the whole world was a figment of gravity's imagination.

"Jeans, I've been thinking. What if words are in charge of the world? What if it's words that makes things real to us, or at least—maybe they're what make us imagine what is real. If that's true, then the most powerful thing in the world you could be is a poet . . ."

"Money is what's in charge of the world," Jeans said.

"We've got money."

"Listen, friend, that liddle stash of yours won't get you much more than a basement apartment for a couple of weeks."

"No, I don't need money. I need to be a better writer."

Just then he saw something blown flat against the glass of a bus shelter. He knew he'd found something. It was a card of some kind. He picked it up.

"It's a library card," he said to Jeans.

Jeans looked at Tom strangely. "Were you lookin' for this?"

"No," Tom said.

"Yes, you was," Jeans said. He smacked him with the back of his hand. "You always sayin' you was just pullin' my leg, but I been watchin' you, and I be damned if you not a Finder like you say. God tryin' to tell you somethin'."

"Like what?"

"Like how should I know? All I know is, the back o' your brain was lookin' for a library card," Jeans said.

"Maybe."

"It's gettin' cold at nights. You sure you don't want to sleep in my nest?"

Tom nodded. "See you in the morning."

"You know you ain't never gonna get enough money for a billboard. You know that, don't you, Tom? I'm tellin' you that as a friend."

They parted to take separate streets.

The Spaghetti Factory was a big empty building with boarded-up windows and crumbling bricks. Tom stood inside the door while his eyes adjusted to the dark. People had lit a few small fires on the cement floor and were gathered around it in quiet groups. Where was all the partying he had expected? Someone bellowed as if he was in pain. It echoed. The place was like a dungeon.

"Tom?"

He turned. It was Janice. She'd lost weight, and her hair was longer. She was pretty now, in a whited-out sort of way. She held something in her arm, and it was a moment before Tom could see that it was a baby doll.

"Welcome to the persons' garbage dump," she said. "Did you come to see Pam? She's over there."

She took his hand. As she led him, she told him how she'd

walked into a hospital one day and picked up a baby and would-
n't put it down.

"So they put me in the hospital, too. Psych ward. They said I
had postpartum psychosis. They put me on these little purple
pills, which I mostly remember to take."

She stopped before a group of kids sitting around a fire. They
were just sitting, smoking, talking in quiet voices.

"Pam, look who's here," Janice said.

Pam smiled a little and stood up. "Hi."

Janice put her doll on her shoulder and moved away.

"You're not going anywhere, are you, Janice?" Pam asked.

"No. I am definitely not going anywhere." She walked away.

Pam turned to the others gathered around the fire. "Guys, this
is Tom."

A boy flicked a cigarette stub into the fire and wiped his hand
on his jacket before he held it out to shake Tom's hand.

"You're among friends here," he said.

"Jeffrey-Jones is a cook," Pam said. "Sometimes he brings us
leftovers from the restaurant where he works. This is Morocco."

A girl nodded and smiled at Tom from the floor. "Hey, Tom,"
she said.

"Morocco is a dancer," Pam said.

"I'm a ballet dancer," Morocco said, "but I'm doing clubs
until I get a gig."

"Dance for us, Morocco," another boy said.

As if he'd asked her to pass the salt, she got up and started
dancing. Someone Tom hadn't met yet started playing a blues
tune with a harmonica.

"That's Rain on the harmonica," Pam said. "Not his real
name. These are all street names. He's good, isn't he."

Still another person began to sing. It all blended together, and
Morocco danced a slow, sad song in the firelit dungeon.

"What's your story, Tom?" Jeffrey-Jones asked.

Tom looked at him blankly.

"He means how did you get here," Pam said. "Everyone has a
story."

Tom didn't know how to answer. All he had was a whole ream of fiction.

"You don't have to say anything," Jeffrey-Jones said. "Everything's freedom here. Have a seat. The fire's free, the warmth is free."

Tom stood stupidly until Pam gave him a little push down on his shoulder. All three of them sat.

"I value freedom," Jeffrey-Jones said. "When I was a kid, my dad would tie me to a chair when I was a bad boy. Last time it happened, he left me tied up and went on a big drunk. When he got back two days later, I stood up in my wet pants and walked out and never went back. That's freedom—you don't care about anything and anything doesn't care about you."

Rain told his story, and Baby told hers. Morocco only danced, so Jeffrey-Jones told her story. Tom listened, but he couldn't relate. He had great parents, a nice home, two cars. His parents were probably planning to get him an old beater for his sixteenth birthday, whenever that was. He wasn't going to sit around an old warehouse all his life. He was going to get an education.

"Tom writes his story down," Pam said proudly when there was a silence. "He's a poet."

It felt good to hear her say it. Was it true? He hadn't found Daniel. The others looked at him expectantly.

Other people were dancing now. The smoke in the factory air was wavy with music and dancing. "I just came to find Daniel Wolflegs," he said.

"Haven't seen Daniel in a while," Jeffrey-Jones said.

Tom stood.

He didn't belong here.

"Tell him I'm looking for him," Tom said.

He turned and walked away.

Pam said goodbye, but he pretended not to hear.

Chapter 9

Youth, do you believe in the tongue's game?
— Act 1, scene 15

Tom didn't sleep for the cold. He rose when it was still dark. He could hear his joints creak when he stood up.

He took the long way around to avoid Samuel. He could see him there on the bench, sitting still as a statue. His hands were in his lap, and he was staring into the river as if his son were going to float by like a message in a bottle.

The Fas Gas washroom was locked. He walked around trying to find another station with open bathrooms, but they were all locked. Finally, he relieved himself in an alley, then went to the bakery.

Someone had gotten there before him. There were a few smeared cardboard boxes lying on the ground. Tom picked them up and threw them back into the dumpster. He didn't want to give the owner any reasons to not share his garbage.

It was too windy to work. There was no sign of Dreadlocks or Tattoo. Tom was cold and hungry when he walked into the library. At a desk with a sign saying INFORMATION sat a big woman wearing small glasses. She was reading a book.

"Can I help you?" she asked without looking up from her book.

"Are poets rich?" Tom asked.

"Poetry section is on the third floor," she said, pointing to the elevator doors.

He took the elevator to the third floor, then found a study carrel near a window. He shivered over the heating vent. When he'd warmed up enough to bend, he put his head down on the desk and went to sleep.

A woman was standing beside him when he woke up.

"The library does not allow indigents," she said.

She was dressed all in black, and her gray hair was piled on top of her head in a bun. She was tall and so thin that all you could see was bones under her dress. She might have been a skeleton but for the skin on her head and hands. Even her hands were bony, crackable.

"What's an indigent?" Tom asked, trying to sound awake.

"Someone with no place to stay."

Tom licked his chapped lips. "I'm not an indigent." He wasn't exactly lying. He had his island.

Tom opened his backpack and slowly took out his notebook and pen. "I want to be a poet," he said.

The woman straightened her spine. Tom thought he could almost see breasts beneath the dress.

"See, I've got this book and this pen—it's hard to explain— but when I write in it things happen . . . I'm trying to find out if poetry is a true thing about me."

"One does not declare oneself a poet," she said.

"Who does, then?" Tom asked.

"Well-read persons with credentials," she said. "People who have the verbal sensitivity, the theoretical background, and the formal training are those who declare who is a poet and who is a fraud." She looked him up and down. "It is unlikely that a person who does not know the meaning of the word *indigent* could be a poet."

Tom felt woozy. He hadn't eaten much in a couple of days, and nothing at all this morning. He steadied himself and tried to focus on something.

"If you faint in my library, young man, I shall be more than angry. Already the other librarians say the only people who come into this section are those who come accidentally or those who want a quiet place to read. If an indigent faints in my section, I shall never hear the end of it."

"I'm fine," Tom said, nodding his head. But the nodding motion made him see black spots before his eyes. He sat down, but the floor seemed to be trying to tip him out of his chair.

The woman vanished, then reappeared. He figured he must have lost time because he didn't see her walk away or walk back.

"Drink this," she said.

"What is it?" he asked, but he started drinking before she could answer. He couldn't tell if it was a drink or soup, but his head cleared instantly.

"Thank you," he said.

"Now, Mr. Poet, you will be leaving."

"I have to stay," he said. "I have a library card." He fished it out of his pocket and flashed it. "You can't kick me out if I'm here to read."

He didn't know if that was true.

They looked at each other. Finally, she said, "Very well. You will not disturb me with any noise or behavior of any kind. And if you are here to read, you will read. You will read what I give you to read."

Tom nodded.

"Come," she said.

She led him to a shelf and pointed to a book.

"That's a poem?" Tom asked, lifting the book from the shelf.

"This is a collection of poems by Christina Rossetti. Here," she rifled through the book. "Read this one. They say it is suitable for children."

Tom took it back to his desk.

The poem was entitled "Goblin's Market."

He read it.

He read it again.

He read it three times, each time more slowly.

The words were things you could hold; they had weight and shape and smell: **fruits, lick, melon, golden.** He wrote some of the words in his book. It wasn't stealing, he decided. It was more like collecting, like stamps or comics. When he read this poem, it was easy to see why his own wasn't working, wasn't finding Daniel, or home.

He went to the librarian's desk. In the corner was a broom with eyes painted on the straw and a little gingham ruffle under the eyes like a skirt. Tom stared. He was pretty sure that the broom had winked at him.

"Did you read the poem?" she asked.

"Yes."

She studied him carefully. "And?"

"I see what you mean about being a poet."

She took the book without looking at it. She was looking at Tom. "You liked it?"

She handed him another book. "Try this. It's modern."

It seemed to Tom that she looked at him almost hopefully.

The modern poems didn't let him in easily, but he didn't give up until he got something. He had to read a poem three or four or ten times before it let him in, before he could squirm between the lines, curve into its o's, hang from the tails of g's and q's, leap from period to period like rocks in a pond. Sometimes he could get between the letters and the page, and see the poem backwards: its opposite. If you didn't give up, it let you in to play. It was like a maze of mirrors, or a Nintendo game. You just had to try everything, and eventually something happened and you understood. Except you could never beat the game. And when you quit the game, you couldn't see the world the same anymore.

From each poem, Tom took a word. If he could just get good enough . . .

He stacked the words one on top of the other like blocks. Sometimes two or three went together in a row. He made houses and bridges and roads out of them. Once he looked up and saw the librarian looking over his shoulder. She was reading his word collection with slightly parted lips. Tom covered them possessively. She put another cup of the warm drink on his desk. "For the poet," she said softly. Shortly after he drank it, he left to find Pam.

Just as the sun was going down, he found her. Pam ran a hand through her hair when she saw him coming. Tom was jealous that she could just run her hand through her hair whenever she wanted. He didn't know how she could stop after just once.

"Are you okay?" she asked.

"Yeah. I got an education today."

"In one day?"

"I read a real poem," Tom said.

"Oh."

"No, I mean a real poem. It was about these two sisters who see goblins at dusk, and one tastes the goblin fruit, and then she's going to die if she can't get more, but the goblins won't come for her after that, and so her sister has to save her life, and . . ." He stopped. "It doesn't sound the same when you talk about it."

"Tom, when was the last time you ate?"

"I could never be a poet like that," he said.

"No. You can be a poet like yourself."

Being close to her like this gave him the courage to speak his fear. "Pam, what if poetry doesn't do anything? See, I had this dumb idea that words were in charge of the world . . ."

"That's not a dumb idea. It's like telling fortunes."

"Yeah," he said. The wind was blowing hard. Any harder and it was just going to blow him right over.

"Tom, when did you eat last?"

"This librarian, she gave me some stuff to drink. It was different. I can't describe it, but it made me feel better for a while . . . You know how gorgeous you are?"

"You're still wearing whatever it was she gave you," she said, laughing low. "You've got a mustache of it."

Tom felt himself blushing and lifted a hand to wipe his mouth, but Pam stopped him. "Here, let me," she said.

She placed her hands on either side of his head. She licked his upper lip, a small quick lick. Tom thought for a moment that gravity had disappeared and he was flying off the world. She licked again, a dry lick, like a kitten, and then again, slower and wetter. And again.

"Mmm, good," she whispered, and she licked it all off and Tom didn't move until she was done and then he kissed her mouth and tasted the stuff again in her mouth and he couldn't stop until Pam pushed him away. He was breathing as loud as a braking bus.

"I was right the first time," he said.

"About what?"

"About poetry, my book. I wrote in it that everything's going to be okay." He kissed her again. He wanted to plant a flag on her. "Pam, do you love that boyfriend?"

She stepped back nervously, glanced around, nodded. "We're having a few problems."

"Listen, if you need money, I've got some."

"That's what he said when we first met."

"I just want to help."

"I don't need anyone's help."

As if speaking of him had summoned him, Cupid appeared with two of his friends. They made no sound. It was as if they were on a high-gravity planet, with no atmosphere for sound. Pam's mouth opened, but no sound came out.

"I heard about this," Cupid said to Pam, "but I didn't believe it."

Tom stepped in front of Pam. Cupid pushed him, hard. He was heavy in high gravity. Tom pushed back, remembering that he could fight. One of Cupid's friends hit Tom in the face. Two of Tom's molars came into his mouth. He spat them out, and they rolled like dice on the pavement. He could feel his mouth filling with blood. Someone kicked him in the back, and another, from the side. He hit the pavement, and his head bounced. No sound.

It was like a movie with the sound turned down. He saw the police car, lights flashing but no siren. Cupid tried to drag Pam away with him, but she ran in the other direction. Then Cupid and the others were running away, not making a sound.

Chapter 10

Now come and play on the flute!
It will guide us along the grim pathway.
Act 2, scene 8

He woke up in a hospital bed.

When the policeman spoke to him, he heard his voice, but as if it was from far away. He looked in alarm at the nurse standing beside his bed. "Barotrauma," she said. "You got hit on the ear so hard that it busted your eardrum. Turn your good ear to the officer."

Tom turned his head.

"Do you know who did this to you?" the officer asked.

Tom shook his head. He could hear gravity seeping in through the tear in his eardrum, leaking into his brain. It was whispering to him, something close by his eardrum, but he couldn't quite get it.

"Who do you want me to call for you?" the officer said, pulling out a notepad.

"Um . . . I can't remember. I must have a little brain damage, too," Tom said. The officer and the nurse exchanged looks.

"Yeah? Well, you're likely to get a lot more if you keep hanging out with those friends of yours," the officer said.

Tom nodded.

The officer was talking, but Tom wasn't really listening.

Gravity was whispering something to him, and he concentrated, trying to hear. Something about the fight with Cupid . . . except it hadn't been a fight. It had been a beating. He hadn't thrown a single punch.

Couldn't he fight? He'd been pretty sure that was a memory . . . No, the memory was of getting punched in the face. He'd just guessed about the punching back part.

He'd written in his book, **Tom can fight.** But . . .

He could hear the voice seeping into his broken eardrum, now. It said: what if it's not true? What if none of the words in the notebook are true?

The nurse left the room and returned in with a tray of steel instruments. The policeman said, "I'll be back shortly," and left.

"What are you going to do?" Tom asked her, knowing he couldn't run with all that gravity in his brain.

"Just cutting off your hair, young man."

"No."

"What, you want freezing for that? It's got tenants. Lice. Stayed at a shelter lately? We'll shampoo you, too, but you kids never do the follow-up treatment, so we'll just shave it off. Be glad it's not scabies."

"Where's the girl they brought in with me?" Tom asked. "Pam."

"No girl. The police saw her, but she got away."

What if it's not true?

As soon as the nurse went out of the room, Tom dressed and left the hospital.

His heart couldn't beat as fast as his feet could run. The sky was lightening from a purple black to a deep gray. The wind began to blow, and the leaves rattled on the branches.

Tom knew every street. He knew where all the regulars slept: War Hero under the skirts of the giant pines at the library; Red Shoe on a bench across from the doughnut place; the one who sniffed glue in the window well of the old CP hotel. The holes and cracks were full of eyes.

Jenks was in his usual spot, asleep on an old blanket he'd spread out on the sidewalk.

He shook Jenks awake, and the old man came up punching.

"Whoa, hold on. It's just me, Tom."

Jenks relaxed. "H'lo, ghost," he said.

"I'm alive," Tom said.

"S'what they all say."

"If I was looking for a ghost, where would I go, Jenks?" Tom asked.

Jenks waved his hands at Tom. His hands were covered in socks. "You like my mitts? Look, there's holes for my middle fingers." He poked the fingers out for Tom's benefit. "That means leave me alone. I know what I say when I'm juiced. Right now I'm dry."

"I will, I will," Tom said. "Just tell me where to find Daniel."

"Told you. Go 'way."

"Acorn told me you know where he is, he takes care of you sometimes."

The old man swore at him and curled into a ball.

Tom squatted to be at eye level with the old man. "Listen, Jenks. Daniel's father's been looking for him for months. He won't eat anymore until he finds his son. When he dies, his ghost is going to find you, Jenks. Now there's a ghost that won't go away when you sober up. Believe me, Jenks, Samuel's a ghost that'll stick with you."

Jenks unfolded himself and looked up at Tom, his eyes wide with alarm. "The dead don't hide under roofs. The dead don't care," he said finally. "Besides, they can't read their street survival guide. Some never could. If you're looking for ghosts, you just look in the shadows. They are alone. Nobody can sell them anymore. Damaged goods. You just go down any old dark street, and you'll see them."

He pointed with his two middle fingers, which poked out from his socks. Tom looked over his shoulder at the alley Jenks was gesturing toward, and swallowed. Jenks pointed again and nodded his head. "Don't worry, boy. You blow on them, they fall over," he said.

"Thanks," Tom said.

Jenks shrugged. "Coulda told you a long time ago."

Tom searched the shadows in the alley, picking his way among broken beer and Listerine bottles, among trash and human waste. He found the dead, the drug dead, the drunk dead, the dream dead. He found them standing, sitting, squatting, sleeping in the shadows of back doorways and dumpsters, tar babies, sucked so far into the street that she gave birth to them again — helpless, crying, hungry, and without language.

The sun was almost up. They shrank from the light.

Tom found one warrior.

Standing tall, hands in pockets, wide-shouldered. He was street lean — not the spa leanness of the downtown workers, but the leanness that looks like it's been dried out in the wind too long, the leanness that comes with long periods of not much to eat. He was standing, just standing. Beside him was a dumpster with the words RIP ROSIE painted in red on the side of it.

"Daniel?"

The young man looked at Tom. "Who are you?"

When he spoke, Tom knew it was Daniel. His voice was like his father's. He was thinner than his picture, and his hair was longer.

"I'm Tom. Your dad, Samuel, sent me to find you. He's waiting for you at the park. He needs to talk to you."

Tom could see the young man translating in his head, sounds to symbols, words to meaning, school English to street English.

"You're the one who's been asking about me," he said slowly.

"Yes," Tom said. "That's me." He realized that he was standing on his toes for sheer joy. He lowered himself, but a moment later he was on his toes again. "Oh, man, you have no idea —

I've been looking for you forever. Your dad, he told me when I first came that I was a Finder, and, well, at first I thought he was crazy, but you won't believe this, turns out I found all this stuff, stuff I needed, like a job, and money and food and, well, it worked like this: if I wrote it, I found it, and I wrote that I was going to find home, but your dad said I had to find you first and then I'd find home . . . . Oh, man, I was getting scared there for a while because I wrote that I could fight and then I got, you know, beat up by this guy, Cupid, so I was starting to think none of it was true and I couldn't write after all and I'd never get home . . ."

Tom stopped. He was chattering. He waited a moment, but Daniel didn't speak.

"It wasn't just for that. It was for your dad, too. He was good to me . . . So, well, if you want to go now, I'll show you where he is. I can't wait to see the look on his face."

Tom reached out to guide Daniel's arm, but Daniel drew back.

Tom felt gravity pull his forehead and the corners of his mouth down.

"He doesn't eat anymore because he knows you're hungry," Tom said. "He gave away his coat because he knew you were cold. He cries for you."

Daniel looked up at Tom.

"He told me about you when you were young, how when you were little you broke your arm and your leg at the same time while you were stunt biking. He calls you a warrior."

Daniel took a step deeper into the shadows.

"I wrote a poem for you," Tom said, trying to keep the panic from his voice. He'd dreamed of finding Daniel, but he'd never dreamed about what he'd do if Daniel wouldn't come with him. "I'll tell it to you, if you'll come."

Daniel didn't move, but he didn't tell him to shut up either.

"It goes like this: This is what to remember: Remember that you were strong and wild when you were a child. Remember all your good dreams. Remember what he did for you, too. Tell him:

this is what you did for me, and this and this. Remember to fight for what you need. Remember that you are a warrior . . ."

He stopped. Gravity was squeezing all the air out of him.

"So? What do you say?"

"Leave me alone," Daniel said, and he walked away.

Tom couldn't move. He couldn't wade in gravity this thick. He wanted to grab Daniel, wanted to tackle him and scream and shake him. But he didn't do anything. He just stood there and let Daniel disappear into the shadows.

Tom walked to the river where he knew Samuel would be. He was going to ask:

Does it count? I found Daniel—does it count? You never said I had to bring him to you, you only said I had to find him . . .

But when he saw Samuel from a distance, sitting on the bench, hunched and cold by the river, his mouth moving soundlessly, Tom stopped.

He couldn't do it. He couldn't tell Samuel that he'd talked to his son and he wouldn't come. Tom folded his arms over his head and screamed through gritted teeth. He didn't know what to do. He didn't know what to do.

What if none of the words were true?

Tom turned and walked away from Samuel. He walked, not knowing what to do or where to go, until he came to the billboard.

The Magic Flute, September 12–15.

From where he stood, Tom could see the electronic sign flashing the date: September 15.

He glanced from the electronic sign to the billboard. Today would be the last performance of The Magic Flute.

Maybe that day when he'd seen the billboard from the tower, he'd made a mistake. Maybe it wasn't a billboard he should have been looking for. Maybe it was the opera, all along.

Tom smiled. Something about that opera had to do with home . . .

It was working! He'd found Daniel, and now he'd find home. It did count! He couldn't think about Samuel now. He had to think about getting to the opera.

It was too late to find a ticket. He'd have to find another way. If there was one time when he had to be a Finder, it was now.

You had to look like you belonged to go to an opera, Tom thought. He knew he looked different from everyone else. But maybe if he thought, *I am a writer, I am a poet,* he could pass for belonging. Poets probably went to operas. Maybe at an opera, though, the less you belonged, the more you fit in. He could pass for a musician, perhaps, or a singer or a set designer. You just had to walk in with confidence.

First he had to find clothes.

He went to the drop-off bin at Sally Ann's. He found a black shirt, and a black jacket only a little too big for him. He also bought an almost-brand-new pair of jeans. They had a cowboy label, but the jacket covered the label. He wasn't sure cowboys went to the opera. He had enough money left over for a pair of clean socks. He'd given up on underwear a long time ago. He couldn't hear gravity in his ear when he was thinking about what to wear.

He went back to the Greyhound station, showered, and put on his new clothes. The shirt smelled a little of cigarette smoke covered up by pine room freshener. Tom wondered how he knew what pine room freshener smelled like, and decided his mom used it in the house. He liked his new look. His father would probably hate the bald head, but he'd have to admit it had a kind of artsy appeal. Everywhere he went he looked for a ticket, but it was a long shot even for a Finder. Still, he was a Finder. He'd found Daniel. He refused to listen to *what if, what if . . .*

Finally, he took the LRT to the Jubilee station. Patrons who wanted to avoid traffic took the LRT. They arrived at the station looking out of place in black and diamonds, looking like they had been cut out of magazines and glued onto a child's crayon drawing.

He was scared. He took out his notebook and read, **Everything is going to be okay.** He felt better.

Tom thought maybe the patrons had money. They looked

bright, clean . . . moral. Half an hour before the performance was to begin, a couple arrived that looked especially moral: moral in their clothes without creases, in their hair that didn't look like it blew or grew, moral skin, moral teeth. Maybe there was something about attending operas that made you rich. Maybe people like that would share.

He approached the couple. "Could you spare some money so I could go to the opera?"

"The opera?" the woman asked as she slowed. She lifted her purse. "Dear?"

"He doesn't want to go to the opera. Give him money and you'll just keep him on the streets a day longer. Grow up and mug you someday." He put his hand on the woman's back and hurried her along.

Tom was invisible to the others that came. If he spoke to them, they ignored him. He found half a bag of taco chips in a trash can and ate them. When he'd licked the bag clean, and all his fingers, he got out his notebook. He'd write a story that began with a boy sneaking into the Jubilee Auditorium. He wrote the boy invisible, walking just below the line of vision, slipping into an empty seat, listening to invisible music, filling his ears with the secrets of money and family. He wrote that he was a fine actor, with a voice that could cast a spell. He wrote until he felt better.

He just wanted to get in. He knew he would find something in there, something to remind him of home.

He walked casually behind a group of patrons as if he belonged, as if he had a right to walk through the doors of the Jubilee Auditorium.

He was in.

No one even looked at him.

He was just as invisible here as he was on the street.

He climbed the stairs. It was more likely that there'd be empty seats in the second balcony. How had he known about second balconies? His parents must have brought him here before! He knew for sure that he would find here what he was looking for. All he had to do was get by the usher.

Once on the top floor, he pretended to gaze out the floor-to-ceiling windows that overlooked the city. The usher took tickets as people came to the door. He hoped an older person would come along who would need help to be seated. No one came along who needed help. Maybe the usher would go away once the show began, and he'd slip in.

She was looking at him, now. He could see her reflected in the window in her navy and gold uniform. She was suspicious. He had to try something quick.

He bent his head and pretended to cry, softly at first, and then audibly. She ignored him at first, and then she called, "Are you all right?"

Tom pressed his fingers into his eyes. "My girlfriend didn't come," he said. His voice was shaking from fear, but it could have sounded sad, too.

"Your girlfriend was supposed to meet you here?" she asked.

Tom nodded. "We've been having troubles." He walked toward her a bit, put his hands in his pockets.

"I'm sorry," she said.

"Yeah," Tom said. "The worst of it is, I paid for the tickets, but she's got them. I've come all this way for nothing."

"Oh, that's too bad. We could check our records—"

"I wouldn't be surprised if she cancelled them without telling me," he said hastily. Tom lowered his head.

"You know what?" she said. "Why don't you just go in. There's some empty seats, and the show's about to start. Who's going to know?" She opened the door.

"Thank you. Thank you so much," Tom said. He didn't have to act that part. He was genuinely grateful.

He slipped through the doors.

Tom was hardly able to believe that it had worked, that he was in. He walked to the railing and leaned over. The musicians were testing their instruments, warming them up. Each had a light over his or her music. The musician was alone in that light, in a little world of his own, round and golden. The flute trilled, and

Tom felt it play his spine, give him goosebumps from his thighs to his scalp. He would find out now about home. He'd found Daniel. That counted, didn't it? He wouldn't think about Samuel waiting by the river.

"One minute to curtain, ladies and gentlemen," said a well-modulated voice. *Modulated.* What kind of awesome parents did you have to have to know a word like that?

Tom turned around. There was one empty seat near the front, someone sick that night, someone who couldn't come and who couldn't find anyone to whom he could give his ticket. Tom sat in the seat as if it were his.

To his right was a large man whose bulk spilled over into Tom's space, and to his left was a woman with a fur coat that spilled over into his space. Tom didn't mind. It was like being in a cockpit, waiting to be launched into space. Any minute now, he would be in zero gravity. Tom took out his notebook and pen. He was going to write down what happened in the opera so he could remember it later.

The music began. Prelude. Tom turned his good ear to the orchestra.

The music was even louder in his bad ear.

It blew over him like a wind. He couldn't breathe in it for a moment. His broken eardrum offered no resistance. He heard in stereo, the hearing and the deaf.

Where the music went, a great bolus of gravity went, pumped into him, forced, taking up space in his veins so that he could feel it moving through him like a huge clot, coming closer to his heart. He would remember everything soon. As soon as the music in his blood reached his brain, he'd remember. Already he knew he'd heard the whole opera before. At school. At school, where he was terrible at English, Mrs. Leonard Mrs. Leonard Mrs. Leonard had given him an extra project on Mozart.

Tom was beginning to remember.

He remembered now that he knew the story of the opera. He took out his book and wrote it down. The man and the woman on either side of him seemed to lean in toward him. He heard the woman whisper, "Critic."

Tom pressed his pen into the paper so hard that it ripped it. He wrote: The prince is lost, he is attacked by a dragon, witches come . . . He couldn't stop himself from writing; he couldn't stop himself from remembering. The Queen of the Night begs him to find her daughter . . . Tom wrote: The prince agrees to rescue the Queen's daughter . . . He is given a golden flute that helps him through ordeals . . . The maiden loves the prince and weeps and sighs for him . . . The prince must prove himself worthy, passing tests of fire and water, tests of courage and love . . . At last the sorcerer gives the maiden to the prince to be his love . . .

Opening act.

The singers began to sing.

Tom put his notebook away slowly, squeezed his backpack between his thighs, and placed his hands on his knees.

The singers had such small mouths, no bigger than his own, and yet huge sounds came from them. Their voices were wise, knew how to go right into Tom's ear, and into his brain and blood. Their voices were beautiful, so beautiful it hurt, so sweet that it pressed tears from his eyes. All his memories were there, in the music part of his brain. The notes, the perfect pointed notes, were moving his memories, jostling them, so out they came, each in a tear, all his life trying to squeeze out of a pore-sized tear duct, one drip at a time.

Tom was very still.

All during the opera he was very still except for the memories dripping from his eyes. As he listened he invented his own libretto.

Mrs. Leonard plays The Magic Flute *one day during free reading. "They say Mozart makes you smarter," she says. Everyone groans, but then they listen. Tom listens hardest of all. He can feel the music reaching inside his brain, where he knows he's smart, even though Bruce says he's retarded . . . Bruce .*

"Can I do my homework in class after school, Mrs. Leonard? While I listen to The Magic Flute*?"*

Mrs. Leonard isn't pretty, but she is nice. She has eyes that really look at you.

"Certainly, Tom, but don't take what I said too literally . . ."

"I need to be good in English. I'm going to write a book someday."

She smiles. Nice smile. She is nice. "I'll do all I can to help you, Tom. Maybe we can work on some remedial spelling . . ."

For three weeks Tom goes to English class to do his homework. His mark goes from 53 to 67. For that Mrs. Leonard gives him a Magic Flute *pen she received as a promotional item for being a season-ticket holder to the opera. One day she gives him the tape.*

"You've worn me out on this," she says, laughing. "I don't think I want to hear it again for a long time. Here, take it home. If you'll do a report on Mozart, I'll give you extra marks."

"Thank you, Mrs. Leonard."

"And Tom, I've got this ticket to the opera in September. I can't use it. I'll give it to you for ten dollars if you want it."

"I do, Mrs. Leonard. I'll bring the money tomorrow."

Tom takes the tape home.

He knows where Bruce keeps his change. Maybe he could take a few toonies without Bruce noticing. He stashes them in his pocket. He'd never done it before, but Bruce was always accusing him of stealing anyway. He goes into the living room to play the tape . . .

Mom's boyfriend, Bruce. He's home, slamming doors, swearing, and drunk. Where's Mom?

"Turn that screeching thing off!" Bruce rages.

Drooling drunk. Danger.

"What the hell is that noise anyway?"

"Opera," Tom says, getting up to turn it off. "I have to listen to it for school."

That isn't a no, but Bruce takes it as a no. He lands a

kick into Tom's back, and Tom goes sprawling into the sound of Papageno singing.

"I'm the one who decides what goes on in this house," Bruce rages. *Tom crawls to the tape recorder to remove the tape, but Bruce's booted foot comes down on his buttocks, flattening him. "Right? Am I right?"*

Tom screams in his own rage, turns, and tries to pull Bruce down. But the boot ends up in his face, and Tom feels his brain fogging up to the sound of flute music.

"You tell the police, and I'll kill you. Hell, and your mother, too. Got that?"

Tom hears the money slip out of his pocket.

"Is that my money? Is that my . . ." Bruce goes crazy. He hits and hits and hits, and then gravity is making Tom choke, pressing him to sleep to the sound of the music of the flute.

Tom waking up, nothing familiar, including the tape that is all pulled out and lying in a tangled ribbon on the floor and Tom hurting all the way up to the pit of his stomach . . .

The curtain was closing.

Applause. Applause!

"Bravo!" Tom cried, clapping so hard that he thought he might fly. He was sobbing. "Bravo!"

He stood, still cheering and crying.

The man and the woman on either side of him stood, too. At first they only clapped, but then they, too, were calling, "Bravo!" One after another, all the patrons stood and clapped. The whole auditorium was cheering. The curtains opened again for the singers to bow. The man beside Tom smiled and clapped him on the shoulder. The woman looked down at him with loving, weeping eyes.

Then Tom turned and ran from the auditorium. He leaped down the stairs, three, four at a time.

He ran out onto the street.

He cried, still running. He hurt all the way up to the pit of his stomach . . .

Then he laughed, still crying and running.

Ha! What a zoid he'd been. Thinking his parents were like the McCulloughs on TV and he was like Trevor, smart and nice. He remembered now where he'd got that YOU'RE NICE candy. Carmen Jones had given to him. She'd given one to everyone in their science class with a smile that said, *This is more about who I am than who you are.* She'd given them out on Valentine's Day and he'd saved it for months. She didn't even know his name. What a zoid.

He stopped running, opened his backpack, got out the pen. He threw it hard. It skittered down the street and stopped against the curb.

Everything changed.

The world changed. He wanted to cry and cry until he threw up his heart.

Tom ran.

He ran to the police station. He knew his name now; he knew now why he'd been afraid to go in. Before he got there, he stopped. He didn't need the police to tell him where he lived or what his name was. Tom Nader. Tomas no-middle-name Nader. He didn't need them to tell him why there was no missing person file on him. He remembered running away three years before and staying at a friend's house until the friend's parents and even the friend got sick of him. He knew that he'd run away so often he didn't have any friends to impose on anymore. He remembered the last time he ran away, he'd camped for a week in Fish Creek Park. He'd always gone home again.

He turned away from the police station and began running again. The pain in his side felt good. His breathing sounded like crying, but he wasn't crying anymore. After a while he realized he was running in the direction of his mom's apartment.

He remembered his mom. She wasn't like Mrs. McCullough on TV. She didn't cook much. She made coffee. She smoked. She brought home burgers sometimes. Tom ate cold cereal for breakfast and supper a lot. Tom remembered when he was little and his mom would look at him. Since Bruce moved in, she never looked at him except through the mirror when she was putting on her makeup. Bounced-off-glass eye contact.

He remembered his mom was a lucky alcoholic. Lucky because Boyfriend Bruce paid for her addiction. She watched TV with Bruce. It seemed that was all Bruce really wanted, a TV-watching partner. Mom would never ask if she could watch anything. They watched what Bruce wanted to watch, and during the commercials she listened to Bruce. Bruce had two emotions: angry and happy. If he was angry, Mom was angry too. If he was laughing, Mom laughed.

She was more like a pet, really. She laid around all day, was excited when Bruce came home, didn't complain too much when she got kicked.

Tom remembered all this as he ran toward home.

Home. H–O–A–M. Was that how it was spelled? It started with a huh-huh-huh sound, like maybe you were going to cry. It started with an *h*. The rest sounded sad, like a groan. H–O–A–M. That must be it.

The closer he got, the more he remembered: that he did poorly in science, and that he almost drowned when he took swimming in phys ed. English was the only class he didn't skip. He remembered that his mom only referred to God when she was mad, that Bruce chewed with his mouth open, and that he had no cousins and one uncle he hadn't seen in eleven years. He remembered that his mom had borrowed his last three checks from his flyer money. He remembered that he was pathetic. P–A–T–H–E–T–A–C.

Tom's memory of his real dad hadn't returned yet, but a block away from his mom's apartment building he knew it was because he'd never had any memories of his dad.

Everything was familiar now — that gas station, this seedy pizza place, the broken sidewalk, the beeping traffic light, this fence that had a growling dog behind it, and this alley where Tony Bienert had beat him up once.

This was home, but he didn't belong. Wasn't home supposed to be a place where you belonged? But as he ran, he realized the worst thing of all—he had belonged. When he was in that apartment, he had been his very own stupid, worthless, bad-speller, invisible self.

He quickened his pace as he came to the apartment building. Faster. He could see the window of the apartment and the flag for a curtain and the light was on and he could smell it even from out here—smell the smoke and the garbage and mostly Bruce, smell him on his skin.

And then the apartment was behind him. Behind him farther, farther, then gone, and he was on his orbit back to the Core.

Tom could see the ghosts now, walking the streets, sleeping on benches, standing on street corners.

He hadn't been able to see them before. Gravity pulled him back, back to the Core. He wasn't running anymore. He was walking. The sound of his feet echoed in the sewers. He wondered about sewers, if there were fumes down there that wouldn't let a candle burn, if there were tunnels down there, mazes, where you could wander your days into years and maybe walk away a hundred times and never go anywhere.

He looked up when he heard someone cursing and kicking at a building. It was Jeans.

Tom stood watching, unable to speak until Jeans saw him.

"They gone, Tom. Took off, and didn't pay us. Two weeks work, and didn't pay us." He scooped some rainwater from a gutter and smeared a few of the lower windows. "That money have been for Gina's ring," he said. He leaned against the building, scouring the skyline for any window-washing cages. He looked at Tom for the first time. "You don't look that good. Somebody tell you we lost our jobs? Come on. Gina gonna have to forgive me the ring, but I saved enough money to buy me a plane ticket. I not waitin' anymore. Time to go. You see me off, okay, friend?"

Tom followed, trapped in the orbit of any passing body.

He remembered everything. He remembered that his mom

used to knit, before her hands got the shakes. He remembered
that she had a pretend diamond tiara from when she was prom
queen as a young girl. He remembered she used to read to him
when he was small, and how silent and white she went when
Bruce first called him a retard.

"Comin' up?" Jeans asked, swinging into his tree.

Tom shook his head. He remembered that he couldn't fight,
not Bruce the boyfriend and not Tony Bienert at school. He
remembered the feeling of getting punched, but there'd never
been a time when he'd punched back. The last time Bruce
punched him, he'd lost his memory.

"You can sleep in my nest when I gone," Jeans called down to
him. "You cannot set inside all day in the winter. Scare the
washen. They call the cops. You not invisible indoors. Yeah, I
know you think you invisible, the way you walk around like you
not scared. Like nobody see you 'cause you not worth seein'. You
should come with me to Jamaica. It so cold here in the winter, it
freeze your invisible self into a big invisible icicle."

Then there was silence.

Tom remembered that no one had ever taken him to church,
but that he'd had a crush on Mother Teresa. Tom's heart was talking to him, but he didn't know body language anymore. It was
tapping out a code in heartbeat, three short, three long, three . . .
but he'd never been a boy scout, he remembered. He couldn't
speak.

There was more rummaging, more silence.

Above him Jeans moaned.

"What?" Tom said to the ground.

"It is gone," Jeans said.

"What?"

"The money I been savin'. Gone."

Coats began flying off the platform.

Tom defied gravity enough to look up. "Did you tell anyone
. . . ?"

There was a thud as Jeans collapsed onto the bare platform. "I
been braggin'," he said. He pounded the platform with his fist.

Tom was loose. The notebook wasn't true. He took it out of his pack and raised his arm to throw it.

He stopped.

He held it tightly for a moment, as if he would squeeze it to death, and then he opened it. He flipped through the pages, read a page, then two.

"Jeans . . ." He wasn't sure if he'd said it or just thought it.

No answer.

"Jeans . . ." He spoke this time. "How do you spell Jamayca?"

Jeans didn't answer. He was crying."Jeans! How do you spell Jamaika?"

"J–," Jeans said with a sob, "–A–M–A–I–C–A. Jamaica."

Tom felt like if he opened his mouth, he'd count to the number blue or cry the color six. "I spelled it right, Jeans," Tom said with awe. Jeans moaned.

Tom climbed the tree. "Gravity is the weakest force in the universe," he said aloud. "Someone is making up antigravity at this very moment."

Jeans was lying face down in the coats. He was a wounded bird: if he couldn't fly, he had to die.

"Hey," Tom said, poking at Jeans. "I spelled Jamaica right—in my book."

Jeans didn't move.

Tom flipped the book open again. "Jeans, how do you spell *everything?*"

Numbly, Jeans said, "E–V–E–R–Y–T–H–I–N–G. Everythin'."

"See? I spelled *everything* right. As in, everything's going to be okay."

Jeans sighed deeply.

"Wake up, Jeans. I think—I think you're going back to Jamaica."

"You finally zoided right out," Jeans said into the coats.

"No. I mean it. Sit up. You're going to—"

"No, I amn't," Jeans said, rolling onto his back. His eyes were still closed. "I can't move, see. Can't work. I got this pain—"

"You're going. Now," Tom said. "I wrote it in my book, didn't I?"

Jeans opened his eyes, but still he didn't move.

"I wrote it in my book. You know what that means." Tom was sure now. He smiled. "Remember what the poem said, Jeans? The one about you?"

Jeans slowly nodded his head. "Said, Jeans bought a plane ticket and went back to Jamaica. Guess you not a poet after all, my friend."

"It said something else," Tom said. "I never read it before because . . . because it was in the space, between the lines and inside the letters."

Jeans said nothing. He looked like he might be falling asleep again.

"Listen. The book says, **Tom, a nice guy, took the money out of his locker, got some extra cash, and bought Jeans a ticket to Jamaica.**"

Jeans looked at Tom. "You steal this cash?"

Tom said, "No. I've been saving."

Silence. Then, "You would do that?"

"It says right here," Tom said. He laughed.

Jeans gripped Tom's forearm. Tom gripped his and pulled him up. "Yes?" Jeans asked.

"Yes."

"Yes?" Jeans asked, his eyes coming alive.

"Yes!" Tom said, grinning so big that his cheeks were cramping up.

Jeans made two fists and roared. He and Tom knocked knuckles. "Don't you worry, Tom. The way you save, you have it all back by the time I marry Gina, which is as soon as her mama can plan the weddin'. And when I get rich, I pay you back, man. You know it for a fact."

Together they went to Tom's locker, and on to the airport.

Jeans flapped his arms around the airport as if he'd fly off without the plane. He smiled and spoke to anyone who caught his eye. At the ticket desk, he said, "Lovely ma'am, I would like a ticket to a seat on the next airplane to Jamaica."

The middle-aged lady tucked a curl around her ear. "You don't have a reservation?"

"No, ma'am. No reservations at all. Jamaica is my home. Got me a girl there name of Gina—"

"I'll see what I can do," she interrupted.

She typed things into her computer and said, "You're in luck. There is a seat on flight Q78 this evening at seven p.m. It will cost you, though."

"No fears," Jeans said. "My friend here"—he gestured to Tom—"he is a poet and thereby is rich. We have cash."

When she asked for his passport, Jeans took it out of his pocket. It was bent and dog-eared. He handed it to her with both hands. "I don't stash this," he said to the ticket clerk. "I keep it close to my Jamaican heart."

She perused it closely. Jeans grinned at her until she blushed and handed it back. "Do you have luggage?"

"No, lovely ma'am."

She handed him the ticket. Tom thought she was positively dewy-eyed when she wished Jeans a good flight.

They both slept in the waiting area until Jeans woke up in a panic, wanting to know what time it was.

"It's okay," Tom said. "You've got lots of time." He bought some snacks, and they talked. He told Jeans what he had remembered about his family. Jeans listened without saying very much, then he said, "Read me that book of yours again."

Tom read it aloud, including his last entry about the opera.

Jeans said, "Sounds familiar, that opera, like I heard it before." He checked the time again, as he did every ten minutes. "Want to know my favorite part?"

Tom shrugged. "I know. It's the part where Jeans goes home."

"That part is good, but besides that, I like the part where he rescues the fair maiden. Fair maidens," Jeans said dreamily. "You are good, man."

Tom stared at his notebook. He stood up.

"Good-bye," he said.

"You're going? Now?" Jeans asked.

"Now."

"But the flight doesn't leave for hours."

"There's something I have to do," Tom said.

Jeans stood up too. "You write yourself a poem like you did for me, okay Tom?"

Tom nodded.

"Do it."

"Okay."

"Do it, man."

"Okay."

Jeans gave Tom a hard, smacking kiss. "I will send you a wedding invitation," Jeans said. "You just get yourself an address and see if I don't." Tom grinned and ran from the airport.

He got back on the shuttle bus and headed back to the Core. He paid the fare for the bus and an extra loonie. He figured if he did that every time, he'd have his fine paid off in a couple of years or so.

On the way back, he read his notebook. He reread his collection of words. A treasure. Right here in his hands, a treasure. Hadn't the librarian called him a poet? Couldn't he spell like a damn? Hadn't he just sent Jeans back to Jamaica? He could spell *decide*. He could decide from now on what was true about himself, his good-speller, good-swimmer, gravity-defying self that had been there all along.

From the window Tom could see a plane taking off. It made his heart fly to watch that plane lift into the sky. What could gravity be if he could make a plane that big take his friend home? He felt like he'd just looked gravity in the face, made eye contact.

He read the notebook all the way back. Every word made his backside smile. He was getting that God feeling again, right there under his wishbone, and he wanted to kiss everyone on the bus.

But there was something else.

Something he had to do to make it true, to make it pure poetry. He had to rescue the fair maiden, of course.

Tom got off the bus and ran to the warehouse. Ran! He was fast! Why hadn't he tried out for track before?

He ran into the warehouse and searched every fire for Pam. He found her talking with Jeffrey-Jones.

"Pam."

Jeffrey-Jones smiled at him, a great, generous smile. "Hey, Tom. Everything okay?"

Tom grabbed Pam and kissed her.

"I have to save you," Tom said. What was he saying? "I mean, yes, everything is okay, or it will be, as soon as I save you."

"All this mushy stuff is making me sick," Janice said. She slapped her forehead. "Oh, yeah, I'm already sick." She put her doll on her shoulder and stepped into the shadows.

Pam was looking at him with a puzzled smile. He didn't have a way with girls, but maybe he did with this girl. There was some true part of himself that didn't have anything to do with Bruce or school or anything under gravity.

Jeffrey-Jones stood up. He was going to say something, then he stopped. He looked around. "Do you hear something?" he asked.

"I hear Tom being a crazy person," Pam said.

"I just saw Jeans off," Tom said. "He's going back to Jamaica."

Pam clapped her hands. "Oh Tom, that's great!"

"But something he said made me think—"

"Something isn't right," Jeffrey-Jones said. "Too much smoke." He called out, "Hey, somebody burning contraband?"

"I wrote you this poem on the bus," Tom said, kneeling down beside Pam. **"This is Pam's future: not a life behind glass, listening to the secrets of mannequins; not a world out of reach, lips pressed against the window; not a world for wanting and wishing, but a world for having . . ."**

Somebody screamed, "Fire!"

A few people laughed. "No kidding!"

Then there was another scream, and another. Tom put his notebook into his backpack. He felt the building breathe out, a low trembling *whoosh*, then a moment of absolute silence.

Then mayhem. Screaming, shouting, crying. Tom could see a straight line of flame stitching the ceiling directly over his head.

From the north side of the building where the entrance was, black smoke rose like a great muscled genie. Pam stood up, disoriented, as if she'd just woken up.

Tom grabbed her hand, but he couldn't tell which direction to go. People were running in every direction. "Janice!" Pam yelled.

"We have to get out now!" Tom shouted into her ear. They ran to the front door, but it had been boarded up. People were shoving and yelling, but the crowd wasn't moving.

A voice bellowed, "Over here!"

Tom and Pam and dozens of other people ran toward the voice. Someone had managed to pry a slat of wood from a window.

"Don't push!" a girl cried.

"Back off!" someone screamed in panic from the front of the crowd.

"I can't breathe!" Pam shouted in his ear. Tom could see people in the middle of the crowd, their eyes round, bulging in panic.

"Come on," Tom shouted to Pam. "They're being crushed. Come on!"

He thought he could see another window. The heat was becoming unbearable; the smoke was choking him. There wasn't any air left in the smoke. As they ran, Pam saw Janice wandering as if she were looking for something. "Janice, come with us!" Pam cried. Tom grabbed her arm.

Janice pulled her arm away. "My baby . . . I can't leave her . . ." She disappeared into the smoke.

Tom couldn't see the window anymore. He dragged Pam. The smoke clutched at his lungs as he felt along the wall.

He found it, another boarded-up window. He began ripping at the board with his fingers. Pam was crying.

"Lie down!" Tom commanded. "Put your face on the floor."

She collapsed to the floor. Tom's hands were bleeding, but the board was coming away. He grunted and cursed and pulled. Suddenly, someone else was helping. Tom heard the wood crack away from the nails and the sound of sirens just as a flaming something fell beside them. The window glass was cracked. Tom kicked at it with his boot, and the glass exploded outward.

"Out!" he screamed to Pam. She didn't move. He lifted her up and pushed her through the window.

He meant to swing his leg over the windowsill. He meant to lift his leg and fling himself through the window—there was air there—he could smell it, taste it.

But somehow he didn't go through the window. He was sinking. The window was getting higher, out of reach, so high that he'd never get his leg over that sill, no way. It was floating up and up, and then Tom felt his head rest on the floor, watching the window shrink into nothingness.

There was air down here on the floor, enough air for Tom to think straight enough to know he was going to die. He hoped they'd stop the fire in time to save his notebook. He remembered his mom, a way-back memory, back to when she loved him more than Forget. That window was just a pinprick of light now. He wished he'd talked to Samuel, told him that he was sorry, that he knew finding somebody wasn't the same as getting someone home.

He could hear the music of the opera, now. His ears were hallucinating. Then his eyes were hallucinating, too, because he could see Daniel Wolflegs, his face close to his, his eyes like a wolf's eyes, piercing the smoke.

"Are you dead?" Daniel asked.

Strange thing for a ghost to ask another ghost, Tom thought. He shook his head.

Daniel smiled, and then he lifted Tom, as if he were made of smoke. Tom could hear sirens, and answering sirens, as if they were speaking in code to each other.

Daniel had his arm around Tom's waist. "Just lift your leg, and I'll get the rest of you out," he said. Sure enough, there was that window, as if it had just appeared out of nothing.

"Come on," Daniel said. "Help me out here."

Tom crushed his face against Daniel's hair. "Your dad will die if you don't go to him," he said.

Daniel swore. "All right! All right!"

Tom lifted his leg with all his strength. He fell out the window, then Daniel fell almost on top of him, and just before the rescue worker came for them they lay together, breathing in sync.

Chapter 11

What joy it will be, if the gods remember us . . .
Act 2, scene 29

Tom and Daniel were given oxygen masks, and someone put a blanket around Tom's shoulders. The ambulance worker tried to give one to Daniel, but he shrugged it away. Over by another ambulance, Tom could see Pam. The red-haired social worker from the youth shelter was beside her with her arm around Pam's shoulders. Tom felt he'd grown inches in the last few minutes. The ground seemed far away.

Tom asked the paramedic, nodding in Daniel's direction, "Is he okay?"

"I think he's all right," the worker said to Tom. "How about you?"

"I'm okay," Tom said.

He was better than okay. He was alive! He could breathe! He could walk—he could up and walk in any direction he chose:

back to Samuel, back to the cops to report an assault by Boyfriend Bruce, back to someone who would help him get back on his feet. He could decide.

The ambulance worker was checking out a kid who had just been brought to him. "This one's a transport," he said to his partner. They loaded the kid into the ambulance. The kid looked about ten years old. He was wheezing like he had an old whistle lodged in this windpipe.

"That was Winter," Daniel said. "He goes home in the summer, when his dad's away on the rigs. In the winter, he stays with us." His voice was drowned out as the ambulance peeled away and switched on its sirens. Tom wanted to write down what Daniel had said about Winter.

The firefighters were laying some things neatly in a row. They were too busy to see Tom and Daniel. What were the firemen doing? Tom thought he was seeing everything through gauze. Maybe he was dreaming.

Tom came closer, until he could see for sure.

Morocco. Rain. Jeffrey-Jones. Laid out side by side.

He knelt by Jeffrey-Jones. He wasn't burned. He wasn't bruised, not that Tom could see. He was perfect, almost smiling, like he'd smiled when he'd told Tom welcome, it's all free.

"You know him?" someone in a uniform asked.

Tom nodded. "Jeffrey-Jones."

"Spell it?"

Tom spelled it. He spelled it perfectly. He just knew.

Tom looked and made himself see. He made himself see that they were dead. This was something you had to remember. Real power wasn't in forgetting. It was in remembering. He would write it down and make people see that here were good hearts. He knew he could do it, knew he could make people see with his words. He knew what words could do now. They could make people see what had been real all along. He hoped Jeffrey-Jones was home now. H–O–M–E.

Pam wailed. They laid out Janice's body, still clutching a melted doll.

"Get these kids out of here," a man with a clipboard ordered.

The social worker led Pam away, and Tom and Daniel were directed out of the cordoned-off area.

They walked away together without speaking. They both headed for the island.

Samuel was standing by the river when they came, his arms limp at his sides, his face crumpled as a blond raisin. He was as lean as Daniel, and Tom could see that Daniel looked like his father, and almost as old.

"Daniel," Samuel said softly.

The old man put his hands on Daniel's shoulders hesitantly, as if he wasn't sure Daniel would really be there. Tom knew he'd be feeling what he felt: skin like paper, and underneath, fragile bones. Ghost bones. Skin as translucent as ghost skin. And dead eyes. There was no light in those eyes. They'd been bounced out of heaven one too many times, those eyes.

Daniel wavered, ghostlike, and Tom thought the boy would have floated away if Samuel hadn't had his hands on his son's shoulders.

Samuel shook. His huge hands lifted to cup Daniel's face. His hand went all the way around Daniel's skull. He felt his son's face with his thumbs, the bones of his jaw, back to his shoulders. It was if he couldn't really see him, as if he were blind and needed his hands to see him with. He bent down and dipped his hand in the water. He washed the soot from his son's face, as if he were an infant. He washed his sores.

"No one sees the river anymore but me," Samuel said to Daniel. His voice was a chant. "I sat by it waiting for you, learning patience. It became my river. Now I give it to you. It is always the river, but the water in it is always new. Do you see, Daniel? You will always be Daniel, but the spirit in you can be new. Come home with me."

Daniel put his hands over his father's. His hair flowed behind him. It seemed to Tom in that instant that the river was rushing too fast for such a slow, sad moment.

"I am sorry, son," Samuel said. His voice was so clogged that Tom could scarcely understand him. "I am sorry. I love you."

They embraced.

When Samuel opened his eyes, he seemed surprised to see Tom standing there still. "You can go home now, Tom Finder," he said gently. "Go home."

Chapter 12

A human being like you. What if I asked you who you are?
Act 1, scene 2

Tom sat down on the curb and stared for a long time at the burned warehouse. The building was crumbled and black. Gray smoke rose limply from the ruin. The bodies had been taken away. Men in hardhats were speaking in groups inside the taped-off area.

A group of onlookers gathered behind him. One of them said, "They start fires in a building that's boarded up and says NO ENTRY all over it, and then it burns down. Surprise, surprise."

The beautiful office workers, their arms hung heavy with all the good business of the world.

"Danger to the whole community . . ."

"Heard of a guy made three hundred dollars a day begging. They probably all got bank accounts."

Account. A–C–C–O–U–N–T.

"No, they blow it all on drugs."

"There you go. A few less druggies to worry about now."

Tom wasn't afraid of voices anymore. The old voices had been like a skin on him, becoming part of himself, turning him into nobody. Layers of scar skin, scar tissue, until he could hardly find himself under all of it.

But he knew something now. If you wanted to know what was true, you had to start with the things you knew for sure, and he knew for sure he could swim and spell and find things. Find anything—like maybe a new life, a new home. The words of his notebook were true. He'd found his own voice under all those layers. Even if he didn't find anything else, he'd found the most important thing: Tom.

"Excuse me, sir," Tom said, turning to the men speaking behind him. Their faces became embarrassed and defiant as they guessed by Tom's smoke-smeared face that he'd been one of the kids in the building.

One of them hitched his briefcase and quickly walked away. Another ignored him.

"Could I borrow a pen, please?" Tom asked.

Two of the men looked at each other, and one reached into his jacket pocket. Wordlessly, he handed a pen to Tom.

Tom smiled at the man and looked the pen over. It was a good one, perfectly weighted in the hand, big enough for a man's hand. "This is going to be good," Tom said to the man, smiling.

He took his notebook out of his backpack. The pages were still damp, but that just made the ink line thicker and bolder. He began writing.

He would write their stories. Everyone of them had a story. The newspaper man would buy it, Tom was sure. And maybe take him home to meet his wife. He wrote their names. Not their real names, but their street names, the ones they had died in: Rain, Morocco, Baby, Jeffrey-Jones, Janice. Tom wrote their stories, there on the curb with his feet on the pavement and his head in gravity.

He had no trouble finding the words.

Other books by Martine Leavitt

The Dollmage

American Library Association Best Books for Young Adults Nomination

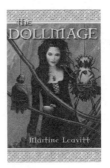

In this intricately woven tale of the frightful effects of love, pride and power, the Dollmage is the wise woman of Seekvalley. As her powers weaken and age comes upon her, she knows she must choose a successor. On the day she predicts to be the birthday of her chosen one, two girls are born: Annakey and Renoa. One must learn the Dollmage's magic, but which one? She chooses Renoa, but as Annakey grows, she discovers that she, too, has magic.

ISBN 0-88995-233-7
CAN 9.95 / USA 8.95

The Dragon's Tapestry
BOOK I OF THE MARMAWELL TRILOGY

American Association of Mormon Letters Award
Canadian Library Association Notable Book

When news of dragon trouble comes from the north, villagers in Marmawell scoff. Dragons haven't flown in the land of Ve for many generations. But Marwen, the Oldwife's apprentice, doesn't scoff. She knows the reports are true; she senses the dragon's magic. But who in Marmawell will listen to her? She has no parents, and she knows too much of the old magic. But worse by far, she has no tapestry, no cloth woven by the Oldwife at her birth and inlaid with symbols of her destiny. To the villagers, she is the "soulless one."

Her destiny will lead her to lost lands, to a powerful magic she can scarcely control, to a mystery no one should have to face alone.

ISBN 0-88995-080-6
CAN 9.95 / USA 8.95

The Prism Moon
BOOK II IN THE MARMAWELL TRILOGY

American Association of Mormon Letters Award

The word is out upon the land: Young Marwen has vanquished the dragon Perdoneg. Minstrels carry her name to the farthest corners of Ve, transforming her lyrically into the heir to the wizard's staff. But her transformation is not yet complete; the staff is not yet in hand. And danger lurks more closely than she dares believe. The wizard's staff is sought by another whose past is intertwined with Marwen's. And what's more, he holds the dreadful power of the Prism Moon to which Marwen finds herself inexorably drawn.

ISBN 0-88995-095-4
CAN 9.95 / USA 8.95

The Taker's Key
BOOK III IN THE MARMAWELL TRILOGY

Canadian Children's Book Centre Our Choice Award, Starred Selection

In *The Dragon's Tapestry* and *The Prism Moon*, Marwen recovered her tapestry, the cloth woven by an Oldwife at her birth and inlaid with symbols of her magical destiny. She vanquished the dragon, Perdoneg, and returned with Prince Camlach.

But an evil sorcery now prowls the land. The Oldwives are losing their magic, drought withers the fields and an ill wind weakens the hiding spell that protects Ve. Worse still, Marwen is powerless to stop any of it. Her wizard's magic drains away, and she has difficulty casting even a simple spell to heal a garden. She must find the key, the powerful talisman whose magic has become her only hope and whose symbol is woven into her tapestry. As evil rumbles like thunder around them, Marwen and the Oldwives must confront the elusive truth of the Taker's Key or never escape the deathlands.

ISBN 0-88995-184-5
CAN 9.95 / USA 8.95

About the Author

MARTINE LEAVITT is the
award-winning author of
The Dragon's Tapestry,
The Prism Moon, and
The Taker's Key, which
make up the Marmawell
Trilogy. Her most recent
novel for teens, *The
Dollmage,* was chosen as
a BBYA (Best Books for
Young Adults) title by
the American Library
Association.